Icing on the Cake

ABOUT THE AUTHOR

STEPHANIE PERRY MOORE is the author of more than sixty young adult titles, including the Grovehill Giants series, the Lockwood Lions series, the Payton Skky series, the Laurel Shadrach series, the Perry Skky Jr. series, the Yasmin Peace series, the Faith Thomas Novelzine series, the Carmen Browne series, the Morgan Love series, the Alec London series, and the Beta Gamma Pi series. Mrs. Moore is a motivational speaker who enjoys encouraging young people to achieve every attainable dream. She lives in the greater Atlanta area with her husband, Derrick, and their three children. Visit her website at www.stephanieperrymoore.com.

THE SHARP SISTERS

THE **SHARP** SISTERS

#5

Icing on the Cake

STEPHANIE PERRY MOORE

darbycreek
MINNEAPOLIS

Darby Creek
A division of Lerner Publishing Group, Inc.
241 First Avenue North
Minneapolis, MN 55401 USA

For reading levels and more information, look up this title at www.lernerbooks.com.

The images in this book are used with the permission of: Front cover: © Andreas Kuehn/Iconica/Getty Images: © SeanPavonePhoto/ Shutterstock.com, (background).

Main body text set in Janson Text LT Std 12/17.5.
Typeface provided by Linotype AG.

Library of Congress Cataloging-in-Publication Data

Moore, Stephanie Perry.
Icing on the cake / Stephanie Perry Moore.
pages cm. — (The Sharp sisters; #5)
Summary: Feeling like the untalented one in a family of five sisters, soon-to-be-sixteen-year-old Yuri, the adopted daughter of newly elected mayor Stanley Sharp, pursues her love of baking and grows in self-esteem when she takes a courageous stand.
ISBN 978-1-4677-3728-9 (lib. bdg. : alk. paper)
ISBN 978-1-4677-4656-4 (eBook)
[1. Sisters—Fiction. 2. Self-esteem—Fiction. 3. Baking—Fiction. 4. Adoption—Fiction. 5. African Americans—Fiction.] I. Title.
PZ7.M788125Ic 2014
[Fic]—dc23 2014003172

Manufactured in the United States of America
1 – SB – 7/15/14

Oprah Winfrey
You are the epitome of what an
entrepreneur should be.
Thank you for going after what you
want with class and vigor.
You inspire me to reach for greatness
and OWN my choices.
The icing you put of the cake of your
life motivates many to strive to be
stellar.
May all who reads this series be the
cream of the crop too.
You are amazing. I am so grateful for
your example…you shine!

CHAPTER ONE
YOUNG

What do you say when all is going right in your world, but you still feel empty? What do you do when you should be so happy, but you feel a little melancholy? How do you act when you're so thankful things have worked out for others, but inwardly you're struggling because you feel worthless? These were my current big questions.

My situation looked like a cupcake that had just come out of the oven, topped with some icing. But as soon as you go to bite into it, because it's a little too hot, the icing slides off.

Yeah, the cupcake is still yummy and you can taste the icing, but something about it just isn't right anymore. You can never put that icing back on top of the cupcake. Actually, that's probably why I felt so gloomy. I didn't feel any way to fix my sadness.

"Come on!" Sloan said to me. "Dad wants us to do the electric slide with him."

We were at an anniversary party for my parents that my dad had given my mom as a surprise. They were two of the sweetest people I knew, and I loved them so much. I knew they weren't my biological parents, but I was so young when they adopted me, you couldn't tell me any different.

There were five of us Sharp girls. I had a biological sister, Ansli, who was older by two years. There were also three girls that the Sharps birthed, Shelby, Slade, and Sloan. Sloan and I were the same age. Our house was a zoo with five girls between the ages of soon-to-be-sixteen and eighteen. Sloan and I will turn the big one-six at the end of December. Thankfully, we all get along good.

I encouraged Sloan to go on. She had really been going through it with my father, thinking he was cheating on my mom. Actually, Sloan had her own issues too. A girl in school made Sloan's life miserable because she felt Sloan was a threat with this boy they both admired. The insane girl nearly damaged Sloan's reputation with a sexting scandal. However, my sister not only came through it stronger, but now my dad was going to help her pursue her writing dreams. I overheard him tell her he wanted to start a magazine with her. While I should have been jumping up and down for my sister, I plopped down in the seat with a massive headache.

"Why aren't you out there dancing?" I heard my mother's calming, yet concerned, voice ask.

I looked up at my mom's pretty face. I just shrugged my shoulders. I tried to smile, but I could never fake it. So I looked away.

As my eyes started to water, she placed her arm around my shoulders, turned my face towards hers, wiped a tear, and said, "Sweetheart, you can talk to me."

"But it's your anniversary party. I don't want to ruin it by bringing you down. You look so happy."

"Well hey, I'm a mother, and if any of my girls aren't happy, how can I be? Share," she said, stroking my hair.

"It's frizzy isn't it?" I said, having a pity party.

"No, your hair is beautiful."

I hated having Indian-type hair. It got so frizzy at times. Most of the time when people stroked my hair it was because I had fly away strands.

"Yuri, talk to me," my mom said as she gripped both my hands and squeezed them tight.

Opening up, I said, "I know I'm just the baby in the family and nobody really expects me to do much, but I want to do something. Shelby has her fashion. Ansli is over there snapping pictures. Slade is about to take the mic, and now Sloan is getting a magazine. Dad is about to be the mayor, and you've been working on this case day and night. I don't want to be angry at them because I am really happy, Mom, but everybody is busy. I have no skills, no talents, and no dreams."

"I actually need some help on my case."

"You do?" I said, as my eyes widened. "What skills do I have that could help you?"

"Yuri, you cook better than me," she encouraged.

"That's because you don't really cook, Mom. But I'm not complaining. Our cooks Ms. Helen and Ms. Susan are wonderful."

My mom winked and said, "And you cook better than them."

I looked at my mom like, don't stretch it.

She smiled and clarified, "Okay you *bake* better than them."

To that I agreed. I loved making desserts from scratch. Always has been my forte. Guess I never saw it much more than as a hobby. How could my love for baking help my mom?

"And you love to go in the grocery store with me. I need helping looking at the expiration dates on a lot of the dairy products. It looks like some stores are knowingly trying to fade the expiration dates off of some products so they can buy them for a very low price and still sell them as if the merchandise is fresh."

"Are you serious?" I said to my mom, unable to comprehend why someone would be so cruel.

My mom frowned. "You're so innocent and precious baby. I don't want you worrying about any of this, nor do I want you so focused on your future. I can't believe you're about to have a birthday."

"See, I'm not good at anything," I uttered, displaying a pitiful look on my face.

"We just said you were the best baker around."

"But how is that a career, Mom?"

"We can figure it out. Now come on, let's hit the dance floor." She grabbed my hand, and we ended the night having a ball.

***

The next day at school felt a little different too. I always walked in with Sloan. We were inseparable for years, but now she had this guy in her life. I didn't want to stand in the way of that, so I went on about my business. I walked around the corner to go to my Family and Consumer Sciences class. Before I could get there, however, I walked up on a mess.

"Your elephant butt better go down another hall," this big guy with a wrestling-chiseled body showing through his shirt said to Logan, a classmate of mine.

Admittedly, Logan was a little overweight. She had trouble fitting through the door, and she sat in two chairs, but she was still a person with feelings. Pushing on her, shoving on her, calling her names, and making her cry was downright cruel.

I stepped in between the tough guy and two girls and said, "What are y'all doing? Let her go!"

"You need to stay out of this," the girl with dreads and a scar across her face said to me.

"Yeah, just let me be," Logan cried out. "You don't know this crew."

"I know they shouldn't be treating you like this. We're going on to class, now." I tugged on Logan's arm, and we walked away.

"You don't know who we are!" This other girl got in my face.

"And you don't know who I am," I yelled back without flinching.

"Why couldn't you just mind your own business, pretty girl?" the tough guy said, playing with my hair before I quickly jerked away.

"You made us an enemy, and now you're going to pay," the scar-faced girl said, as she pounded her fist into her palm really hard like I was supposed to be terrified.

"Come on. Let's get to class," I said to Logan when they were gone.

"You don't know what you just did. They're in the gang Oynx. They'll kill you." Logan motioned for me to check them out. "Look, their bandanas are their mark."

I looked down the hall and saw that they all had on black bandanas on different parts of their bodies. This was serious. Though I did what I thought was right, I exhaled, thinking I might have started my own personal war.

Twenty minutes later in class, I was supposed to be cutting carrots. I was almost about to chop my hand off. I was shaking so bad because I was nervous. When my teacher, Ms. Jenson, started to help another student, I picked up my phone and sent a group text to my sisters.

I texted, "Does anybody know who the people wearing the black bandanas are?"

I got several quick replies. Shelby texted me, "That's the gang Onyx."

Ansli texted, "Stay away!"

Slade hit me back and wrote, "Yeah, don't even go near them."

Inquisitive Sloan texted, "Why'd you ask?"

At that point I started hyperventilating, truly not feeling good at all. How could I stay away from a gang I had already crossed? And what was a gang doing at our upscale Marks High School?

"Answer Sloan's question, why don't you already?" Shelby texted back.

"Girrrl, have you said something out of the way to them!?!" Slade asked with a bunch of emphasis. "Yup, that's it because you're not texting back. What class are you in?"

I still couldn't respond. Sloan texted back, "She's in Jenson's room . . . 212."

That girl had my schedule stored. I did need them because I was in a mess. I must have looked like the color had gone from my face because Ms. Jenson came over.

She put her hand on my shoulder and said, "Yuri, this isn't like you not to finish preparing a meal. You okay, dear?"

I just shook my head. No way was I anywhere close to being alright. There was a knock on the door, and when all the boys started whistling, I knew Slade was there. Why she dressed so provocatively, I didn't understand. She was so beautiful. But she showed just enough cleavage that it was acceptable for school. Yet at the same time, she showed just enough that it was appealing to the guys.

"Excuse me, Ms. Jenson, can I see my sister for a second?"

Ms. Jenson walked me over to the door and spoke to Slade. "I don't think she's feeling well. Will you let me know if she needs to go to the office?"

"Yes ma'am," Slade said as Ms. Jenson went back into class and shut the door. "Okay, uh, what's going on with you? Sloan said to tell me everything too. I know y'all like to keep stuff from me, so I won't scold you, but this is creepy, you talking about Onyx. Somebody gets a hold of your phone and sees their name in it, you could be in trouble just for that."

"I'm already in trouble with them. I pushed them off of this girl, Slade," I said, wiggling my sister's arm for help.

"You did what? You got in the middle of a fight? Why? You're the shyest, little wimpiest thing around. Why'd you do that?"

Stomping, I said, "Because they were picking on this girl, Logan, and she's so sweet. Okay she does have an extra couple pounds that she's trying to lose, but I *had* to help her. She was getting picked on, and it reminded me of kindergarten."

"When you were getting picked on because your chicken pox scars took forever to go away?" Slade squinted and asked me.

"Yes, the scars all over my face just felt like people thought they could laugh at me or something. I hated school and myself after that. I knew how she felt. I didn't realize they were in a crazy gang. They told me I'm in trouble. Slade, what does that mean?"

My sister just hugged me tight. When I pulled away, she reached out and hugged me again. She squeezed me extra hard.

"So does that mean that I'm really in trouble? Oh my gosh!" I said, pacing. I was not feeling any better physically.

"Okay, you've got to calm down."

"I'm gonna die," I shouted.

I was a little too loud, and Ms. Jenson came rushing to the door. "Yuri, what is going on?"

"I need to take her to the office, Ms. Jenson. Can we have a pass please?" Slade asked.

Ms. Jenson scribbled on a piece of paper and handed it to Slade.

We headed to see the coolest principal in the world. Dr. Garner happened to be friends with our dad. Usually, I could talk to him, but at that moment, I couldn't speak for myself. I was looking over my shoulder even though we were in the office. I was so paranoid, but Slade held me up and explained everything that was going on.

"Well, until they do something wrong, I can't just kick them out of school."

"But they threatened my sister, sir. You need them to kill her before you take action?" Slade asked, before I gave her a horrified look. "I'm just saying. I'm not saying they're really going to kill you, but I'm just telling him he needs to do something before that happens."

I hated being the youngest sister because sometimes I just didn't think straight. I let everybody else think for me. The one time that I tried to put on my big girl panties and help somebody else out, I might have signed my own death warrant.

"How bad is Onyx?" I asked Dr. Garner.

He shook his head. "I want to get them out of my school, that's for sure. I suggest you use a buddy system. Don't go anywhere by yourself. Definitely keep a low profile, and I'll be watching the situation. I hear your sister, and she raises a good point. I can't make you a sitting duck, but because there is no recording of them threatening you, hearsay can't really do anything. But you're going to be okay."

Slade looked over at the Keurig machine in Dr. Garner's office. "Could I get her some hot tea, cocoa, or something?"

And when she said that, I brightened up. Dr. Garner was called out of his office and told us to take a second for me to collect myself.

As Slade fixed me something to drink, I said, "You think everything's going to be okay right?"

"Yeah, just like my showcase. I've got to have one for my music soon. I'm trying to put the whole thing together. When you're the record company, it's not just like an artist comes and preforms and goes home. No, I'm in charge of the guest list, getting press there, the reception, having some hors d'oeuvres, and I can't even find a caterer," she uttered as she handed me a cup.

All of a sudden, I wasn't caring about Onyx at that point. I was caring about me and my opportunities. Slade had given me cocoa and hope.

"Let me help," I blurted out.

"Help me how?"

"Let me cater it. Make it a dessert social.

Mom was just telling me I make the world's best cupcakes. They're pretty and yummy. It'll save you a ton of money," I said to her.

"Hmm, I might need to get you stressed out more often," Slade teased. "What you gonna charge me to make it?"

"I'll work within your budget," I said, before I knew I needed to up the ante. "I'll go under budget."

"You're hired."

I put down my cup and embraced her. "Thank you, Slade. Obviously, I need something positive to channel all of this crazy energy."

"We're not a match for a gang," Slade said as she put her hands on my shoulders, "but we are your sisters, and for someone to mess with the baby of the family, they're going to have to come through the rest of us. And to add insult to their injury, we're the last girls they might want to be thinking about messing with. Particularly, if they want to stay in operation. You know what I'm saying? Don't worry. But don't mess with them again. Alright?"

I nodded, as I picked up the cup and drunk

up. She didn't have to worry. I was the baby of the group, but I learned quick, fast, and in a hurry. No more messing with Onyx, and I just prayed that they would not mess with me. But no need to focus on that. Now I had my first catering gig. I was excited. I was growing up. I was proud of me.

***

The day that I had been waiting for—the chance to allow many to taste my cupcakes—was here. I had been baking for two days straight, getting ready to feed the hundreds of guests coming to Slade's new artist's release party. Shelby and Ansli couldn't help me. Shelby was helping the artist's dress. She was the stylist for the day. Ansli was setting up to photograph the important players who were coming to the event, as well as get pictures backstage.

Thankfully, my mom and Sloan were there for me. I think I was getting on their nerves though. I was obsessing about everything.

"Be careful. The box is fragile. We've got to set them down in the trunk just right because if they tilt over, the cupcakes are ruined."

"Ohhh, Yuri, they look so delicious. I just want to taste one," my mom said. "Red velvet, caramel crunch, cheesecake, key lime, and vanilla . . . you go girl."

"Mom, don't even think about touching any of them," Sloan said, seeing our mom truly unable to resist. "Or your daughter is going to lose her mind."

Shelby was kind enough to have her boyfriend create me a logo. Yuri's YumYums looked so cute and delicate. There were two stands that displayed the logo, and I had a professional-looking sign that went in the front of my table.

When we arrived at the back of the location, there was another truck that was unloading all types of desserts. I looked at Sloan, and she looked back at me. She seemed confused. This cute blonde-headed dude was taking in many desserts.

"If she was going to get somebody else to do this, she just should have told Yuri," Sloan said to my mom, saying everything I was feeling inside.

In a calming voice, my mom said, "Well, we don't know. Maybe they have more people, maybe she wanted more than just cupcakes. Clearly they've got an array of desserts over there. As I've taught you girls, it's usually not a perfect world."

When my mom saw the sign of the truck she said, "Oh, that's the lady who has a shop not too far from the house. Treats by Ms. Pinky."

"Yeah, but mom I thought I was the one providing refreshments," I said, barely hiding my disappointment.

"Well, you are providing refreshments, Yuri. Don't get caught up in the fact that you're not doing this solo."

"Wait 'til I find Slade," Sloan said in an upset tone.

"Come on, let's hurry up and get set up. The event starts in less than an hour."

When I saw all of the tables and set ups and booth coverings they were pulling out for Ms. Pinky, I didn't want to go in. Sloan saw me sitting in the car extremely intimidated.

As she approached my mom rolled down the window and Sloan said, "Mom, can you go and find out where her table is going to be set up."

"Oh yeah sure," my mom said, scurrying away.

"You can do this," Sloan tried to encourage.

"Yeah, but look at all that stuff that lady has. I'm going to look like a kindergartner compared to a professor. Nobody is going to want my food. Look what they're pulling out now: little, individual miniature glasses with pudding and stuff inside."

Sloan put her arm around me to comfort me and to tell me I could do it. It was all going in one ear and out the other. The more and more I thought I could, the more stuff Ms. Pinky and her crew were taking out of the truck. I had a few different flavors of cupcakes, whoop dee do. She had cookies, slices of cake, pudding, mousse, pie, ice cream, and, of course, cupcakes too.

"Mom said I need to come and get you guys and show you where your table is," Slade opened the car door and said.

Sloan grabbed her collar. "How could you do Yuri like this?"

Slade yanked back. "Do her like what?"

"Not tell her that somebody else is going to be serving," Sloan said, folding her arms.

Slade rolled her eyes. "Because it's my show, and I didn't think it was any of her business. She asked for an opportunity, I gave it to her."

I frowned. I could not believe they were talking about me like I wasn't there. True, I wasn't as strong as them, but this hurt.

"Oh, what? You thought you were going to be the only one?" Slade said, looking at me like that was the craziest idea.

"Look, you're new at this, and I'm giving you a chance. I can't believe you're giving me grief when I got to get out there and win people over with this song. Support me today. It's not about you, Yuri. I'm making you a part of this. You'd think you'd be grateful, dang," Slade said as she started to walk away from the car window.

"You could have told her about it," Sloan said before Slade got far away.

"What was I supposed to do? This is my partner's aunt's restaurant. I'm helping my sister out, her aunt wants to help us out. It's all family. Get over it, get your stuff out here, and set up," Slade demanded. "And I've got to get ready for a show. I can't believe y'all are giving me drama."

I got out of the car, and the blonde-headed guy came right over. "Hey, I'm Paris. Can I help you bring something in?"

"No!" Sloan coldly said to him. "We have arms. Come on, sis."

We grabbed some stuff and went inside. My space had nothing on it but two little stands. A sign to go in front of the table wasn't going to make it an inviting space. This Ms. Pinky lady had a true booth. It looked like a store on wheels. Even though people weren't going to have to pay for my stuff, I wouldn't want it compared to hers. I knew Sloan couldn't babysit me forever. Once we got all my stuff inside, it looked as cute as it possibly could, but it was still less in comparison to Ms. Pinky. Sloan was supposed to be doing a write up of the event so it could be one of the first articles in her magazine.

"Go, I'll be fine."

"You're okay," she said, completely feeling pitiful for me as she looked over at the magnificent booth. Mine looked like a kid's lemonade stand.

"Can I try one of your cupcakes?" Paris said.

I felt so out of place. Many were at Ms. Pinky's sweet set up. He probably would be the only one who would come over the whole evening, so who was I to tell him no.

"These are yummy," he said, after gobbling down a vanilla cupcake and a red velvet one.

"Thanks."

Then I heard a whole bunch of laughter. My dad was visiting Ms. Pinky's booth. He walked her over to where I was.

"This is my daughter. One day she wants to have an operation like yours. She's so talented," he bragged to Ms. Pinky.

"Oh, isn't this booth precious. Paris, I see you over here tasting. Is it yum yum like her lil' logo? Of course you've got to say so. You don't want to hurt her feelings," Ms. Pinky gloated.

That was such a rude comment, I thought. I wanted to snatch my cupcake from Paris's mouth. I didn't need him to lie. My food was good, and I knew it.

Paris walked into her trap. "It is yummy."

If he expected me to thank him again, that was over. I wanted him and this rude lady to leave me be. Paris saw I was anything but happy.

"I hope your sister and mine won't be too nervous up there," Paris said, trying to lighten the mood.

"Oh, so you're Charlotte's brother?" my dad asked.

"And I'm her auntie. Sometimes I claim her," Ms. Pinky joked.

My dad suggested, "Cool. Well, it'd be great if my daughter could come work with you. You can help her learn the ropes."

"I'd love that," Ms. Pinky said as she and my dad walked back over to her station.

I did not ask my dad to plead my case with Ms. Pinky. She had looked at me so condescendingly. The last person I wanted to help me was her high-tooting behind. But they made a deal right in front of me. Who was going to say no to helping the mayor-elect's daughter? Ms. Pinky wasn't. She saw an opportunity, and she was all over it. I wasn't happy with it at all, and Paris could tell.

"My aunt can be a little brash," Paris said.

"You think?" I said to him.

"But she means well."

"I'm sad I'm even here," I uttered to the stranger.

He put his hand on my hand and said, "But you look cute in your apron, your food tastes good, and you're here. How many people can say they've got a business at your age? You're what? Sixteen?"

"I'm not sixteen yet."

"Well, don't be so hard on yourself. My aunt is old. You're just getting started. You'll surpass what she's doing in your lifetime. Learn from her. Learn the stuff she's doing right and things she's doing wrong. Be better than she is. But don't beat yourself up about it. You're young."

CHAPTER TWO
YOKED

"Wasn't the show great? Aren't you so proud of Slade?" Sloan came over, shook me and said.

My sister's performance was amazing. The song "Be My Friend" was hot, and her singing partner, Charlotte, a cute blonde, could hold her own too. The rhythm and blues mixed with pop rock sound that the two of them had was electrifying.

They looked cute, and I knew that's because Shelby had hooked them up. Sloan was bragging that her magazine issue was going to be dope because of all the great pictures Ansli had captured. Everybody was contributing, but me. Sloan was bummed with Slade for not making me the sole dessert person, but she quickly left me to be bummed out alone.

Every time someone came from the crowded room to the back to get some refreshments, they didn't come to my little area. I went over to Ms. Pinky, and I looked like a fool feeling sorry for myself. I guess my face showed my disappointment.

Sloan put her arms around me and said, "After everything I just went through, this might not be an ideal situation for your cupcake business, going up against a guru in the dessert field. But nobody's laughing at your effort like they laughed me out of school."

I shook my head. I knew my sister meant last month when she went through a terrible ordeal with a girl who was jealous because a boy she liked, liked my sister instead. But this wasn't the same.

"But at least you were vindicated when it all came out. Nobody's eating my cupcakes! I shouldn't have even been here."

"Yeah, but a naked picture of me is still floating around on somebody's phone. I promise you. Since we put that heifer in jail, I doubt people will go around showing it, but they're probably getting their little peeks on, and I'll never be able to live that down. But you don't see me wallowing in what I can't change."

"Dad wants me to work with the lady."

"Well great! If she's on a level that you're trying to get to, what's so wrong with that?"

"Yeah, what's wrong with that?" a male voice came from out of nowhere and said. Sloan looked at me and gave me a smirk.

I turned around and said, "Okay, don't get no ideas."

"Look at the way he's devouring you with his eyes. Don't dismiss the interest."

She was such a writer. There was no happy ending happening. I had no interest in the guy.

"It's rude to eavesdrop," I said to him.

"I just came to get another cupcake, and I overheard the two of you guys." Paris winked.

"Oh, Yolanda dear, come here," Ms. Pinky said in an uppity tone.

"It's Yuri!" I yelled out.

"Okay," she said in an uncaring voice. "Come here, dear."

Sloan and Paris stayed at my booth, not that I needed someone to manage it when no one else was coming by, but they guarded it as I stepped over to Ms. Pinky's world of delightful treats. Seeing her setup up close and personal, I really was in awe. Not only did she have an array of items, but the presentation was spectacular. Tiers of desserts just calling your name.

"So your dad wants us to work together. He thinks I can help you," she said. "I'm not really for charity."

"Charity?" I said, truly offended.

"You know, helping those whose skills are way beneath mine. But in this case, of course, I'll make an exception with your dad about to be the mayor and all. I just wanted to let you know I do have expectations. You got all your cupcakes mixed all in together, and because of that, some of the frosting from one flavor is on another. An absolute no-no. You must keep all of the same cupcakes together."

"But that's your opinion," I said in a humble tone.

"No, if you're going to be working with me, that becomes your fact. I think the whole point of you shadowing me is to learn how to do things the right way. If your father thought it was wise for you to continue with presentations that look a mess, then he wouldn't have asked for my assistance. I can sense a little resistance and jealousy, actually, on your part. Sweetie, it'd be foolish of you to think that you can walk in my shoes when you just started out in this business. Now granted, I was never as bad as you are when I first started baking, but I wasn't grand either. So, there's hope," she said as she reached over and patted me on my head. "Here's my card. On there is my email and my cell number. Please text and email me your schedule so that I'll know when you're coming. I don't like surprises, and I can't have too many workers in the shop at one time."

I started to say "Anything else, your highness?" Instead, I just looked at her like she was a witch. While I didn't really know her, all indications so far proved my theory was true.

"Toodaloo, that'll be all," she said, as if I was invading her space.

Slade was coming back out on stage to give special thanks. I walked back over to my booth and listened as she said, "Just want to thank you all for coming tonight. It's hard to start a dream, but your support has made it so much easier. Charlotte and I are truly grateful. While we're still trying to come up with the name of our group, the single is going to be a hit because you're going to tweet about it, tell the world about it, and buy it when it hits the shelves. I'd also like to thank my parents for helping me create a record label. Also, I thank Mundy Records for granting me a distribution deal. We're going to make you proud, sir! I'd like to thank my sisters, especially Shelby for helping us look fabulous, Ansli for capturing the moment, and Sloan . . . you better write a good article about tonight, sis."

"I will!" Sloan yelled out.

Slade continued, "Oh, and I gotta thank

Ms. Pinky. The desserts are fabulous. Thanks for everyone coming. One thing I've learned is that when you're supposed to be at a place for a certain number of hours, you can't go over or it'll cost you. So I don't care where you go, but you gotta get out of here. Bye! Goodnight everybody!"

I couldn't hold back the tears at that moment. My sister didn't even thank me, and Sloan didn't even realize that I'd been left out the acknowledgments. She rushed out to Slade to hug her. There I stood alone. Well I guess I wasn't alone when someone put his firm hand in mine and squeezed it tight. I wanted to jerk away, but I couldn't. He knew what my family didn't. I felt worthless.

***

My sisters and my mom were all by the stage cooing over Slade's excellent performance. Having a pity party had never been in my nature, but that was because before I'd never wanted to do something great myself. My first attempt at it, I'd failed miserably. I was in the back, pitifully looking on.

"So can I have your number or what?" Paris asked.

"Don't you need to go congratulate your sister or something?" I said, not wanting to be rude to the white boy.

He wasn't my type, not that I even had a type. I never had a boyfriend, but when I had fantasied about who I'd be with, a blonde-headed, blue-eyed, preppy boy wasn't what came to mind.

"I saw you earlier. Who do we have here?" my dad said as he came back over by my stand.

I looked at Paris like, "Uh-huh, just like you walked away when he came over the first time with your aunt, you might wanna walk away now because he is not going to go for me talking to you." It wasn't at all about a color thing. It was about the fact that I was the last Sharp sister without a guy, and if my parents were going to stay sane, they'd want to keep me their baby. Staying their baby meant I was to have no boyfriend for a long time, and that was just fine with me. Clearly, I had other things to focus on. If I wanted a future and if I wanted to be dynamic like my sisters, I needed to get my act together. "I'm Paris, Charlotte's brother. I just was telling your daughter here how delicious her cupcakes were."

I started coughing. That was such a pitiful line. Clearly, I had almost as many as when I came in, so obviously my stuff wasn't that good.

Looking Paris up and down my dad voiced, "Okay, well thanks for introducing yourself. I'm sure Yuri appreciates the compliment, but your aunt probably needs help cleaning up. I'll help my daughter."

"Dad, you don't have to do that," I said.

"No, I want to help you," he insisted while starting to gather my containers.

"But you don't have to."

He awaited direction and aid. "I know I don't have to, but I want to."

"I'm just going to throw the cupcakes away," I said to him.

He frowned. "No you're not! These are delicious."

"How do you know, Dad? You haven't even tasted them!"

"I taste your food all the time. These can't be any different. So what a few of them got turned over on my way in here and look a little less than desirable? I know they're still delicious. I'm about to head to the homeless shelter to thank the people there for their support in the campaign. I'm sure they'll appreciate these cupcakes. You wanna come?"

"Sure, why not?" I said as I looked back up front and saw the rest of the women in my family having a party without me. "I'm going to go tell Mom I'm going with you."

"Mmm, okay," my dad said in pain as he clenched his chest and fell backwards a bit.

I rushed over to him. I was beyond scared. Paris saw my dad falling. The two of us grabbed both sides of his arms before he fell.

My dad sighed, "Don't make a big fuss out of this. I'm fine. Grab me that chair."

Sitting him down, I said in a panicked tone, "Oh my gosh! I'm going to tell Mom."

Before I could turn to fully walk away, he grabbed my arm with whatever strength he had left and said, "Don't you dare tell her about this.

I told you, I'm fine. I'm fine!"

"Okay," I said, sensing he was absolutely angry.

"I'm sorry, sweetie. I didn't mean to snap at you. I just want to make sure you don't go worrying your mom. Look at her over there. We just had our anniversary party. Just got through this major election. She's proud of you girls."

"She's not proud of me," I said, making the moment about me when it shouldn't be.

My dad could tell that I needed him to prove to me that he was okay. He sipped on some water while helping me pack up. I felt it was too soon, but he had already put me in my place once. I wasn't going to push him. He knew his limits, and, hopefully, he was just tired from all the running he'd been doing.

I was glad I was going with him to this event because I was going to see to it that he spoke, and then we got right home. When we relaxed in the limousine, he had his eyes closed, but he still had an uncomfortable look on his face. I placed my head down and started praying he was okay. The last I needed or wanted was for something to be physically wrong with my father. He was right. He'd come through so much. He had to just be tired.

We pulled up to the homeless shelter. My dad had the driver wait around on the side. We went inside. He was greeted by many cheers.

He took to the podium and said, "I would not be mayor-elect today if it had not been for you guys spreading the word to the people you know in Charlotte and actually getting out and voting yourselves. I stood before you and told you that I planned to make a difference for all citizens in this great city. While we won the first battle of getting elected, I am not going to defer from that goal. I'd like to set up a time to come back and hear your concerns, your dreams, and your stories. We can collectively figure out a way to get you back on your feet. I'll be sending some people through here with resources, jobs, and more food to show you that you're not alone. Tonight I actually plan to start with my daughter Yuri. She's a baker. Though her cupcakes have been through a lot this evening, I promise you when you eat one, you'll be fighting for another one. Yuri, why don't you—" before he could say "come up here," my dad completely fell down.

The director of the shelter and I ran to the stage. No way was this happening again. He had to get up.

"Is something wrong with your father?" the director asked me. "Is he sick?"

"He was bobbling earlier, but he said he was fine."

"No, he's not fine."

My dad came to and said, "Just get me to a chair. I'm fine."

"Dad, you're not okay!"

He was taken to the director's office, and he sat on the couch for a while. There was a doctor on staff at the homeless center that just happened to be there finishing up checking on some of the residents. My dad didn't allow me to come in and hear all that was going on, but when the director came out, I grilled him.

"Is my dad okay? What's wrong with him? Do we need to call an ambulance? Is he going to be fine?" I asked the doctor.

The doctor patted me on the head and said, "Yes, yes. You breathe before we have to take you to the emergency room. Your father's going to be okay. He does need to go and see his regular physician. He promised me he was going to do that, but he'll be okay. He's just dealing with a lot."

My dad came out of the office looking exasperated. He smiled my way. Naturally, I smiled back, so thankful he was okay. The director and a couple of the men who lived at the shelter helped my father out.

When we got to the car, my dad said, "I know this seems scary–you not knowing what's going on with your father–but this has gotta be our secret."

"Secret? No way, Dad."

He gripped my hand and said, "Listen, you're my baby girl. You and I have always kept sweet secrets."

I laughed, "Yeah that you ate more dessert when Mom told you not to have anymore."

"And you ate dessert when Mom told you not to have anymore," he said.

"Dad, that's harmless stuff. How can I keep this away from Mom? Obviously something's wrong. You heard the doctor."

"I'm fine. Don't get me all worked up. I just need some rest. I'm going to go see my doctor. Everything is going to be fine. You've gotta promise me you're not going to say anything. Too much is on the line. Okay?"

I was my dad's baby. There was no way I could go against his wishes. Certainly, he knew his own body. So I told him, "Okay, I won't say anything," knowing that I had partnered up with him in his lie. It just didn't feel right. It felt so wrong.

***

The next morning, I rushed down for breakfast, after waking from a nightmare that my dad was gone. Reaching the bottom stair, I was thrilled to hear his voice. He was talking to my mom. Still I had to see with my own two eyes that he was okay. There he was smiling at me with an apron around him, fixing pancakes.

"You want some, baby girl?" he asked, giving me a nervous look.

To ease his mind, I went over to hug him. He was okay. I had proof in my arms.

"You're acting like you haven't seen your dad in forever. I don't get a hug like that?" my mom said as she extended her arms.

I went over and hugged her too. My dad eyed me and made sure I said nothing about his condition the night before. I winked his way, reassuring him again, though I felt uneasy about it.

"The rest of your sisters are sleeping. I did not want Slade to have that performance on a school night. I knew they were going to be too tired. They better get on up," my mom said.

"She said she got it cheaper on a school night. That's our business women. The girl is taking after her mother," my dad teased before he looked at my mom. "Honey, you better go and get them up."

"You're right," she said, knowing she could make us move like no other.

As soon as the coast was clear, I said, "Dad,

are you going to see your doctor today?"

"Listen baby girl, I don't want you bringing anything up about that. You see, I'm fine. I just needed some rest."

"But you're not answering me, Dad."

He kissed me on the forehead, handed me a plate of pancakes, and started whistling. Darn, I was mad at him. I huffed, sat down, and started gobbling the food.

My mom was the best at getting us up. She didn't come downstairs alone. All four of my sisters were with her, and they were fully dressed.

Shelby, Ansli, and Sloan were playing around. Slade wanted to get to school. She was actually the last person I wanted to ride with because I was still upset that she had Ms. Pinky cater her event, but I wasn't trying to be tardy either. I had a test in chemistry, and getting to school early to study was just what I needed.

As Slade and I rode in the car, she played her song over and over. I mean I could understand that it was brand new. It hadn't even hit the airways, and she wanted to make sure it was on point. It actually worked out pretty well because she had it on, so we didn't have to carry on a conversation.

When it ended the fourth time, she finally turned it off and looked my way. "Last night was hot, huh?"

I looked out the window, gave her no energy, and uttered, "Yeah."

"What's up your butt?"

She did not want to go there with me. It had always been that Shelby, Slade and Sloan had more attitude than Ansli and me. We were real quiet girls compared to the three of them. But at this point, if Slade took me there, she was going to see a side of me that she'd never seen.

Slade thought on it and said, "Oh, so cat's got your tongue? I know you were not thinking that I was going to have somebody else with food there. Like I told you when you first got there yesterday, it wasn't my intent, but you know, it worked out anyway. Everybody loved her stuff. And plus, you were all cute back there, and Dad says you're going to be working with her."

"When'd you talk to Dad?"

"Before the event was over last night, we took a break."

"How'd he seem to you?" I asked, wondering what she thought of his condition.

Had she noticed that he was weak? Had he shown any health issues in front of her? If so, I knew Slade wasn't going to be able to keep it. I truly hoped she noticed something.

"He seemed fine to me!" she yelled like I was a lunatic for probing.

"You don't have to raise your voice, Slade."

"Well, you don't have to seem ungrateful, Yuri."

"You didn't even tell me that the lady was coming. We talked about cupcakes. You didn't tell me she was baking everything else."

"What else can you bake?" Slade sarcastically said as we pulled into the parking lot.

"I don't know, but I could have tried."

"Exactly, you could've tried. I needed a professional. I mean you still had a lot of cupcakes back there. Ansli felt so sorry for you. She told dad to have you take it to the homeless shelter, but I think you were throwing it out or something, huh?"

"No, we took it to the homeless shelter," I said, feeling really low and now understanding where my dad got the idea.

Slade parked and stared my way. "Look, it's taken me years to get a record company interested in my work, and while my new label is just distributing my songs, I've realized that I've still not arrived. I'm closer than I've ever been. I wasn't upset with those who did have a deal. Instead, I gave them my full support, bought their albums, downloaded their songs, and watched their videos over and over because I'm studying them, trying to figure out how I could step up my own game. So whatever issues you have with Charlotte's aunt, you need to get over them. She's the best at what she does for a reason. Maybe you spending time with her can help you find out why and help you be better too. That's all I'm saying. I gave you a chance, and you got the nerve to be mad at me. Whatever. We're at the school. Get out."

"You're not gonna drop me off at the front?"

Slade huffed, "No. Walk like I have to. Ungrateful self."

We both slammed both doors. I was trying to hold back the tears. My sister and I were at odds.

Before I went to my class, I went to the girls bathroom to fix my makeup. It was still early. I was shocked when I heard crying coming from the stall. The crying was getting louder and wouldn't go away, so I knocked on the door.

"Are you okay?" I asked.

"Go away." I could tell it was Logan's voice.

"Logan, it's Yuri. Please come out. Talk to me. You can come out, please." When she did, I was surprised to see blood by her nose. "What in the world! We gotta go and take you to the office. This is horrible! Let's get help."

She grabbed my arm. "No, no, no. I just need your help cleaning it up."

"Is your nose broken?"

"No, it's just blood."

"How'd this happen?"

"Don't ask. Did you see anybody by the door

when you came in? Are they gone?"

"I wasn't even paying attention. I was a little upset myself."

"Oh my gosh! They could still be out there. Oh my gosh!"

"Those Onyx people? What do they want from you?"

She shouted, "To join. I said no, and it's the worst mistake I've ever made in my entire life. They've been torturing me ever since. This morning I was a part of the knockout game."

"What!"

"I told you too much already. Please just leave me alone." Without even wiping her nose, she grabbed her stuff and ran out of the bathroom.

As soon as I went out of the bathroom, I saw the same three jerks who had been around before. One male, two females, but thankfully Logan was far down the hall. She didn't need anymore drama.

One girl with short hair that made her seem like a boy, pushed me hard. "You got something to say?"

"If I had something to say, I would say it," I

said back, knowing that I did have something to say because they shouldn't have been punching on Logan, but I wasn't going to say that.

"Oooh, she's getting all smart."

When I saw Slade, I rushed over to her. "Oh, so you wanna walk with me in the halls now?"

"There're those people I was telling you about," I mumbled under my breath, alluding to the Oynx members.

Slade put her arm around me. "They're the leaders of the gang. Let's walk fast."

My sister made sure I was calm and secure in my class, before she took off. Mr. Newton, my chemistry teacher was helping a few others. So I sat and studied on my own.

Sitting in chemistry class twelve minute later, I could've choked. The two girls, the one who pushed me and the other one, were in my class. It was time for our test, and the two chumps were sitting right behind me. I had studied, but the essay questions were giving me pause. I had answered to the best of my ability and looked back over my test. I turned mine in first, and the two girls from Onyx turned theirs in right behind me. I don't know, I guess I thought all gang people were stupid, but for them to finish so fast and appear so confident, maybe I had underestimated them. I wished that I could talk to them and tell them that there had to be a better way.

But before everyone was finished taking the test, Mr. Newton called us out into the hallway. "You all have the same answers."

My eyes bucked wide. I hadn't copied off of anybody's paper. But there was no way I could accuse the two of them for cheating off of mine. If their gang was as dangerous as everyone was telling me they were, that was the last move I wanted to make.

"So nobody is going to tell me anything?" he said. "Alright. Let Dr. Garner handle it."

About twenty minutes later, I was pacing back and forth in Dr. Garner's office. When he opened the door, I rushed to him and said, "Sir, I did not cheat off anybody's paper. It's those girls. They cheated off of mine, but I can't—"

"I know, I know, I know. I believe you," he said.

"So you know they're dangerous?"

"I'm looking into all of that. I don't want you to go and say anything you can't take back. But let's just say, I want you to stay far, far away from them. There's some stuff going on here that's really disturbing, and that crew is a crew with whom you do not need to be yoked.

CHAPTER THREE
YES

"Dr. Garner, I understand I'm not supposed to be around these gang kids, but what am I supposed to do if I see them beating up on somebody innocent? My parents didn't raise me to turn away when somebody is in trouble," I said to the principal.

"Well, then you need to scream out for help. Under normal circumstances, we wouldn't want you to leave somebody who's in need of assistance stranded. But this Onyx group is around here wearing their pants ultra-low, with these black bandanas draped across every piece of their bodies . . . they're ruthless. I've already had two of my tires slashed this year."

"Are the police involved?" I asked.

"Absolutely, and some might be involved the wrong way."

"I don't know what you mean."

"I don't want to explain anymore. I can't be so scared of this group that I don't do my job. I'm the principal here. That's what I get paid for. You're the student. You need to stay out of it and for sure away from this group. You understand?" I nodded while he wrote me a pass. "Here. Get on to class."

As soon as I stepped out of Dr. Garner's office and into the office waiting room area to cross through to exit, the two Onyx gang members stepped up to me and locked the door. One girl had a tattoo I'd never seen before on her cheek that said *Lady G*, so I assumed that was her name. She was real feminine looking, but still looked sort of tough. The other girl almost looked like a boy, with cornrows going straight back, with a build like a linebacker and a look on her face like she wanted to devour me.

"Tell me what you think, Tiny," Lady G said, revealing the bigger girl's name. "She rat us out or what?"

"I don't know," Tiny said, whose name certainly didn't fit her body type. "But if she snitched, that pretty little face she got is going to be real messed up."

"Hey! What y'all doing?" Dr. Garner yelled out and the two of them stepped aside. I was able to unlock the office door and rush out of the office.

The period was about to be over, so I went to Sloan's class to catch her as soon as the bell rang. When she came out, I grabbed her. I was shaking.

"What's wrong with you?"

"It's that Onyx gang. I'm in trouble! Tell me you'll help me! Tell me you'll stay with me and fight with me if they mess with me! Please, Sloan! Say you'll help me."

My sister put her arms around me and said, "Of course I will. Why you think they gon' jump you?"

As soon as she asked the question, a couple

of other suspect members of Onyx walked by and gave me the evil eye. Scaring me further, one guy was pumping his fist into his palm over and over and over again. That confirmed that I was in trouble.

Sloan pushed me to a corner. "What is going on? What happened? I thought you got the message to leave them alone?"

I wanted to say it was a long story, that I wished I could go back and figure out what I did wrong, but I worked on instinct. I was there for Logan. I simply went to class and some people cheated off my paper. Why was *I* now in trouble? I truly didn't understand. So I probably looked real shell shocked.

"Well, we are going to need back up. You just lay low the rest of the day. Don't egg them on, and don't leave out of the school building by yourself. You don't have to worry," Sloan said, making me relax.

"I won't. Thank you, Sloan."

"Hey, Yuri, wait up!" I heard a familiar voice call out to me.

I turned and saw that it was Paris. I turned

back and kept walking. I had too much stressing me out as it was.

"Wait up!" he said, jogging to catch up with me. "You gon' do a brother like that?"

"You're not a brother," I said to him. "And trust me you don't want to be around me right now."

"Why?" he asked.

Showing little interest, I said, "Well, it's not because you're not looking good and smelling good. That's for sure."

"So then what?" he questioned.

"Seriously. I've got a mark on my head. You don't want to be around me."

With all seriousness, he tugged on my arm, stopped us from walking, stared at me, and asked, "What are you talking about? So the Onyx people are messing with you too? I'm sick of them, man!"

"You know about them?" I asked, relieved, yet more scared at the same time.

"Yeah, they jumped one of my friends last month."

Paris didn't offer more information, and

I didn't want to know how bad it was. It was understood that it wasn't a good thing. For sure, I was gonna stay clear of the defiant group.

Gently stroking my arm, Paris made my heart skip a beat when he uttered, "Don't worry, I'm not going to let them hurt you."

"Paris, please stay out of it," I said as I dashed to class. I didn't want to see him possibly getting hurt by being roped into my madness.

The school day was ending way too quickly. I didn't want it to end, but 3:05 p.m. was upon me. Stepping out of my last class, I smiled seeing all four of my sisters standing outside my classroom door.

Sloan came to me and touched my cheek. "Word's out you're in trouble after school."

"But we got you," Slade said.

"Yeah, they'd have to take on all of us," Shelby replied.

"Hopefully there won't be any trouble, so our help won't be needed," Ansli said, thinking what I was feeling.

I knew our parents didn't like it when Slade got to fighting with some random girls that were jealous of her back in October. If all four of them fought for me, this would be bigger than that. Also, my dad was just a candidate for mayor then. Now, if a gang was going to jump the mayor-elect's daughters, it would be big time news. I couldn't let them risk that much for me. Besides, I didn't want to fight anyone either. As we walked out of the school, two of them were on one side of me, and the other two were on the other side. So many people were giving me looks like I was a pariah. Sloan was on my left.

I leaned to her and said, "Now I know how you felt."

"What, with all the stares?"

"Yes," I explained nervous as all get out.

Sensing I was having a hard time, Sloan encouraged me. "Do like I did, just hold your head up and keep it moving."

"Just need to call Dad," I said, wanting his help. This was blowing up way bigger than it needed to.

Shelby was on my right and said, "Now, what's that going to do? He can't come every day. We've got to face this. Deal with these punks. We need to show them we're not going to be intimidated."

When we walked out into the parking lot, we were overwhelmed, spotting twenty kids with black bandanas around some part of their body. The five of us didn't stand a chance. My teeth started gritting on their own because I was so tense.

Along beside us was a whole bunch of white kids I didn't even know. I looked up and was so surprised to see Paris, Charlotte, and a bunch of their friends. Dr. Garner and other administrators were also nearby.

As the Onyx crew walked away, Lady G yelled out, "This ain't over, Urinade."

It was clear who she was talking to. All I could do was hurry up and get in the car and be relieved because, for the moment, it was over.

***

I couldn't believe I had to go to Ms. Pinky's shop. My dad was serious about this whole internship thing. She was rather smart-mouthed when I met the first time, and I knew she was still brash.

"If you want to learn from the best," Dad said. "You've got to spend time with the best. So get in there, smile, and take in everything she has to say. Learn from Ms. Pinky, and be grateful for the opportunity. Do not go in there thinking you know it all."

"Yes sir, Dad," I said as he dropped me off in front of her place. As soon as I wanted to turn and say, "Aren't you coming in to break the ice?" he pulled off.

"Well, here you are! And there goes your dad," Ms. Pinky said in an unhappy tone as she met me at the doorway.

Ms. Pinky, who was dressed in a business suit, looking more ready to go to a corporate job than head to the kitchen to bake, walked outside. She was talking to the air, fussing to the wind, and complaining aloud about how dare my father not come in and speak to her. Yes, she wanted to get cozy with the mayor-elect. I knew it. My dad probably knew it, which is probably why he didn't stay, but she didn't like it. When she came back inside, she had no problem voicing it.

I wasn't concentrating on what she was saying, not because I didn't care what she had to say, but because I was in awe of the lovely sight in front of me. Seeing her beautiful shop, I just couldn't believe it. Not only did it smell fresher than ice cream, but the pinks, purples, and turquoises throughout the place made the store so inviting. The chairs were dainty. The white countertops appeared almost eatable themselves. Topping off my excitement for the decor were the glass displays showcasing scrumptious-looking treats. But even with all that, it wasn't a large place.

Frustrated, Ms. Pinky yelled out to me. "Well, don't just stand there looking all crazy. Let's get to work! Go wash up. There's an apron in the back. We must get ready for the health inspector. Chop, chop, Missy." Ms. Pinky rolled her eyes and trotted off toward the back. There was a red-headed, female employee in her mid-twenties checking me out. I smiled her way to break the ice.

Guess that made her think I was cool because she opened up and joked, "So, you're here to learn from Cruella de Vil? You sure you wanna work for her?"

I was skeptical with the worker being so forthcoming. I didn't know her. My parents had always taught me to be diplomatic and never say anything that you can't take back about someone. In addition, I was taught to never cosign with somebody who is saying something negative about somebody else, even if you agree.

"I'm Yuri," I said, holding out my hand and intentionally not answering her.

"Hey, I'm Rhonda."

"Nice to meet you. How long have you been working here?"

"Too long," Rhonda said, pointing to the clock. "I'm ready to go now, but I've got three hours left."

"Rhonda!" We heard Ms. Pinky yell from the back. "Why'd you open up the new milk?"

"Because the other one had a bad date on it," Rhonda said boldly and sarcastically like Ms. Pinky was asking a dumb question.

M. Pinky screamed back, "You did what? Rhonda you know the rules! I'm deducting your pay. Yuri get back here, let me show you! Maybe you won't be as stupid as that nut I've got working for me.

"She thinks I'm gonna help her kill folks? She's crazy," Rhonda uttered flippantly.

"What do you mean?" I asked. But before Rhonda could answer Ms. Pinky yelled out again.

The uptight new boss of mine, screamed out, "Yuri! How long does it take to get back here? It's just five steps! And don't let Rhonda fill your head up with lies. I'm trying to save the business here. Customers will be alright."

I opened up the swinging door and said, "I don't know what you mean. Customers will be alright? Do you sell outdated food?"

"So I go a couple days over the expiration date. Nobody's dying from it. I do that with a bunch of my ingredients here. I'm not the only shop, so don't look all bent out of shape about it." She said as my eyes widened with fright. "Now quit looking around. Come here. I need your help."

"Yes, ma'am, what do you need?"

She opened up the refrigerator. "The health inspector is going to be here in a second. I need to switch out this stuff. Put the right dates all lined up nice and pretty in a row, so when they check everything, I'll be in good status."

In my mind I wanted to tell her, "*Are you serious about this? You want to put the right things out only to pass a test?*" But I said nothing. I just followed her out the back door to her car, and when she popped her trunk, she had all new supplies with current dates. We took the out-dated supplies that she was actually using and put them in her car.

Ms. Pinky proudly explained, "When they leave, we'll switch it back out. I'll go to my house and put these newer ones away, and then I'll use them next month or the month after that."

The lady was really insane, and when she heard the chime on the door, she smiled. "Great. We finished just in time. And not a word of this. No one outside of folks who work here knows our little secret."

I wasn't naïve enough to not understand that some people did cheat their way to the top. I guess I just never imagined they did it in the dessert business. When something looks scrumptious and you try it, it's not supposed to harm you.

Ms. Pinky went into sweetie-pie-mode. Watching her interact with the health inspector and his assistant was a joke. Knowing who she really was, I hated watching her being all fake. Clearly the people knew her because they laughed together.

While Ms. Pinky schmoozed to make herself and her shop appear perfect, I stood over with Rhonda and asked, "Does this happen all the time?"

Rhonda leaned in and quietly told all to me. "You ain't seen the half of it. Every night she takes what we don't sell, and instead of throwing them away, she puts them in the refrigerator. Yeah, she'll take off the old icing. But to make them look all pretty and fresh again the next day, she nukes it in the microwave and then puts the frosting on before she serves it. She never cooks a new batch until the old ones are all sold. Now that's not what her sign says, but that's the truth."

The sign in the window read, *Made fresh daily*. Hearing what Rhonda was telling me let me know Ms. Pinky was a bigger fraud than I thought. I couldn't believe Rhonda and I both knew Ms. Pinky wasn't operating right, but neither of us were saying anything to the health inspector.

What was happening to me? I wasn't a shy girl. I stayed in my lane, maybe because I stepped outside of it helping Logan when she was in trouble. I decided not to ever go down that path again—like telling my mom about my Dad being sick or telling the health inspector about Ms. Pinky's trifling, illegal ways. I knew my reasons, and I knew I'd probably never forgive myself if something happened to a consumer. Ms. Pinky taught me my first lesson, and it wasn't that cutting corners was the best way to go. Oh no, she taught me that you can dress it all up to make it look all good, but if it's bad on the inside, it's rotten. Though she was smiling from ear to ear when the health inspector handed her a score of 99, I hoped she would not continue to get away with this. Some kind of way, I was going to have to get out of being under her. I already thought she was slick, now I knew she was slimy. Not the type of person at all with whom I wanted to be associated.

After the coast was clear, she turned to us and said, "Oh, a 99 girls! Thank you both! Stick with me Yuri, and I'll show you how it's done."

I didn't know Rhonda well. However, when she looked at me and I looked at her, our thoughts were aligned, like we'd known each other forever. Ms. Pinky was crazy if she thought I wanted to stick with her. There was absolutely no way. But when she handed me a broom and handed Rhonda a mop, I realized I was stuck until I figured out a different plan.

***

"We haven't had any customers today. Why are we sweeping and mopping?" Rhonda looked at Ms. Pinky .

"Because I'm paying you. I'm going to the back to bake for the catering job. It's not like I'm doing nothing. You need to do what I say. Besides, I've got to take off and go get my kids. It's tough being a single mother," Ms. Pinky said as Rhonda mouthed those exact words behind her head. "I see you, Rhonda." Ms. Pinky quickly turned around. "I've got eyes in the back of my head, Yuri. Watch this one. I'll be back in a few!"

"But, what if somebody comes in?" I asked, not knowing how to take care of a customer.

"Rhonda will tell you what to do. But whatever you do, don't throw away any products."

She didn't have to tell me that. I'd already gotten that message. She wasn't going to throw it away. She was going to reserve it, figure out a way that it could stay on the shelves and be available for customers until it was sold.

When she trotted off to the back, Rhonda vented, "I gotta find someplace else to work. Ms. Pinky was telling me that your dad's about to be the mayor. He can hire me as a janitor. I've got to get out of here!"

"So why do you stay if you don't like it?"

"Because, she's one of the best pastry chefs I know. I'm gonna be in the back. I'm trying not to be here all night. I've got to finish this catering order."

"What if somebody comes in?"

She gave me a five second lesson on the cash register. Rhonda rushed through every step. I was smart, but I wasn't as smart as Sloan. She could pick up anything. I needed to hear fast info a couple of times. However, Ms. Pinky called Rhonda, and my helper jetted to the back.

"But I don't know what you just told me!" I shouted out.

"It'll come to you. Besides, nobody is coming in," Rhonda said as we both heard the door chime.

I bent down so Rhonda would have no choice but to help me. Rhonda rushed back over where I was. I was super thankful she had my back.

I was confused, when Rhonda uttered, "Oh, it's just you. Help her. I've got work to do in the back."

Standing to my feet, I smiled seeing Paris smiling back at me. "You?"

"Yeah, me. I work here in the evenings some days," he said.

"You mean your aunt actually pays you?"

"No." He looked at me, and we both laughed. "So you figured her out already, huh?"

"There're some things I'm figuring out about her that are real suspect."

"I don't want to talk about her anymore," he said as he came around to a side by me.

His eyes held interest. Butterflies were swirling in my tummy. When he placed his hand on mine his were cold, so I jerked away.

"Sorry."

I playfully popped him in the gut. "Yeah, you're freezing."

"It is December, you know," Paris replied. "What's going on with you and Onyx?"

Exhaling, I got serious. "I don't know. I guess I put my nose someplace where it didn't belong, and they're not going to let me forget."

"Well, hopefully they'll back off knowing you got more friends than they counted."

"Yeah, hopefully." I looked down.

I heard him blowing on his hands. Then I felt his finger under my chin. He turned my face toward his. His hand wasn't so cold anymore, but the warmth in his eyes drew me in.

He whispered, "I don't want you to be afraid."

Stepping back, I said, "I didn't want you to get other people involved. I mean, I'm thankful you did, don't get me wrong. I'm so grateful, but I feel terrible about this. My sisters, you guys, y'all just came from out of nowhere, and this can get really ugly."

"It could. But this is bigger than you, Yuri."

I shook my head. "I don't understand."

"A lot of us came from the same school last year. When the gang first started, people were getting seriously hurt. We don't want that to be the same case at Marks. If we don't stick together, then we're all in trouble. It'd be you today and somebody else tomorrow. So don't feel bad we're involved."

"I just hate there's really nothing we can do. My dad's about to be the mayor, your dad's the superintendent of the schools, and it's just like we're darned if we do and darned if we don't. You say something, it gets worse. You don't say anything, it's getting worse. I don't know what to do." I threw up my hands, and he put his around my waist.

In his embrace, he mesmerized me when he said, "Maybe we should just forget about that and focus on something else."

"I don't know what you mean," I said, completely bashful at that moment.

"Let me take you out on a date."

"You drive?" I asked him, remembering he was also a sophomore.

"No, but I know people who do. Let me worry about that. You just say you'll go out with me."

I paused for a long while, and then I heard Rhonda's voice from the back. "Say yes, or I will!"

Paris and I both let out laughter. He was a cutie. I wanted to rub my hands all through his smooth, blonde hair.

"Do I need to go ask her?" he finally said, but I wouldn't let him move when he tried to tug away. "So you'll go out with me?"

Feeling better than I had in a long while, I said, "Yes."

CHAPTER FOUR
YIELD

I was so happy when the weekend came. No more school until Monday, and no more Ms. Pinky for at least a couple of days. I still wanted to talk to my mother about how upside down my life seemed, but when I went in to talk to her, she was heavily involved in a case.

"Come on in, baby," she said as she motioned of me to come sit.

Shaking my head, I said, "No, I see you're working."

She put down her pen. "I've always got time for you."

"You're so sweet, Mom, but we're so selfish. Always needing your time. It's the weekend; you're working. Obviously you're on a deadline, so I can come back another time."

Before I could leave, she got up and stopped me. "Are you excited about your date?" Earlier in the week I asked her if it was okay if I went out with Paris. Since I was going out with Slade, her boyfriend, Charlotte, and her date, my mom was okay with it. I hadn't seen my dad around for much of the week, but because my mom had signed off on it, all was good.

"Are you nervous about it? Shelby said she took you shopping after school the other day so you got a cute dress. I hear the plans are to go to a tree-lighting celebration and dinner. You don't seem excited? You don't feel any pressure from this guy do you?"

My mom was going in so many different directions. The attorney in her was coming out, and she was doing her investigation, probing trying to figure out what was wrong with her baby girl.

So, since I was that important to her and I really did need her advice I said, "When should a person stay out of other peoples' business even when they know the information they have is life threatening?"

"Well, if it's that dire, then you need to come to people you trust," my mom said as she squinted.

Trying to calm her, I shouted, "I'm not saying it's me!"

I could tell she didn't believe me, but, grinning, she said, "Oh, okay. Well whoever it may be needs to come to someone they trust like their parents. Seriously, Yuri, is there something you want to talk about? Something you need to say? I know I've been a million miles an hour. It seems over the last few months, you girls have been going through so much."

My mom was right. If it wasn't Shelby being caught in the middle as her boyfriend dealt with a domestic violence situation or Ansli having to deal with a homeless boyfriend, it was Slade mixed up with some guys dealing drugs or Sloan uncovering all kinds of corruption going on at school. Now it seemed to be my turn. I had three big things on me. I was scared for

Logan. I was petrified of Ms. Pinky's ways, and I still was really worried about my dad's health.

Before I could figure out a way to just talk to her, Sloan busted in her office and said, "There you are, Yuri! Come here, I need you to see something."

"Well, let it wait for a minute, honey. I'm talking to your sister."

"It can't wait, Mom. It can't wait," Sloan screamed in a panic.

"Is everything okay?" she asked Sloan. I wondered the same thing.

Sloan nodded, but the panic was all in her face. Something wasn't right. So I kissed my mom on the cheek and followed my sister upstairs to her room.

"What's going on?" I asked.

Sloan pointed. "Look, online."

"What am I looking at?"

"Read it," she said as her body started shaking like she was having a conniption.

My sis had me worried. I looked at the screen. I held my breath, seeing there were several negative comments floating around out there about Logan from her being a freak to her being an imbecile. It just was stupid nonsense, but the negative posts were growing.

The last one said, "She'd be better off dead than to show her face back around Marks High School. Marks is no place for sluts."

"But then look at this post from Logan," Sloan said, pointing to the computer screen.

My heart dropped when I saw the words Logan had typed "I'm done."

I couldn't hold back the emotion. It was the weekend, and I didn't have Logan's number, but, instantly, I needed to talk to her. I needed to make sure what I was assuming she was saying wasn't really how she felt. Helping her was what I had to do.

"I got to talk to her. I got to calm her down. This isn't good!" I squealed.

Sloan bellowed, "For sure you're right. This isn't good."

"Is she going to take her own life, Sloan? Oh my goodness! Why are these people being so mean on here?" I asked as my eyes watered.

"People who know they can get to you, they gnaw and pick until you have nothing left. You know I learned that going through that stupid scandal."

My sister was right. She had always been a tough girl, but having naked images of her floating around the school made her feel like worthless. But she kept her head up high, and we Sharp sisters supported her, and she got through it. People really felt bad for her when it was all revealed that she didn't even take the picture of herself. Sloan texted a couple of other people. Somehow my sister got Logan's home number.

As soon as I dialed it, I heard a male voice say, "What now?"

His harshness made me barely want to speak, but I mustered up the strength because I knew I needed to. "Can I please speak to Logan?"

He shouted, "You leave my daughter alone!"

"Sir, I'm a friend of hers," I said, hoping that would make a difference.

"Yeah right, a friend? Who are you?"

"My name is Yuri Sharp. I go to school with

Logan. Can you please tell her I want to talk to her?"

"No! And don't call this house again!"

"But sir, I need to make sure she's okay!"

"Don't call this house again," her father barked, slamming the phone down in my ear.

I got off the phone even more worried about Logan because she had to live with that tough man. No telling what thoughts were going through her mind. But there was nothing I could do. I just had to hope she was going to be alright.

***

"Come on, Yuri. Avery's here!" Slade knocked on my door and screeched out.

Avery was my sister's boyfriend, and while Slade could sing, Avery could blow. He actually had a record deal with Mundy Records too, but his was not just for distribution. He was their new up-and-coming artist. His new single dropped the month before, and it was blowing up.

"Come on. Come on!" Slade pounded and said again.

"She's coming, goodness," Sloan told her.

"Yeah, I got to make sure baby sis is just right," Shelby said, as she tweaked and tweaked and tweaked on my outfit.

I had to admit, I looked fly. Sporting a black, short, leather skirt, some black tights that had a design on them, sweet, funky wedge boots, and a sweater shirt that Shelby created that hung just low enough to be cool and just high enough to be sort of sexy. Slade was getting so upset because my door was locked. My sisters knew they weren't turning me loose until they were ready for me to go, and Ansli stood at the door once Shelby was finally done and snapped tons of pictures.

"It's not like I'm entering into a fashion show or anything," I said to them.

"You're going on your first date. We've got to capitalize on this moment," my sister said to me as she hugged me tight.

Ansli whispered, "Mom and Dad would be so proud."

I knew she meant our biological parents. We very rarely talked about them, but every now and then, when it was a special moment, we both connected . . . hating that they weren't there. I probably moved past it a little bit more than my sister. She was a couple years older than me, so she remembered our parents more than I did. She also took it pretty hard when she learned that they didn't just die in an accident. When we did more digging, we learned that my dad was depressed when he got released by one of the NFL teams for taking steroids. Somewhere along the way that messed him up. He became angry, bitter, and depressed. He took my mom's life and then his. As I pulled back from Ansli and saw the tear in her eye, I knew she was thinking about all of that. But we were okay now. We were still alive, and we did need to make them proud and remember the good.

Finally when we opened the door, Slade yanked me out of it. She was running and not letting go of my arm. We almost tripped going down the stairs.

"Slow down," my mom said to both of us, dipping her head to the left so we could see we had company.

There was her date standing at the door. I guess Slade thought he was in the car. She stopped running down the stairs then. My sister was all smiles, looking at the hottie who was becoming a rising R&B star.

"You both look lovely," Avery said, making us both blush.

Slade reached in and gave him a big hug. She looked back at our mom before exiting and winked. My sister liked this guy. The smile in his eyes made me know she had feelings for the right one.

"Take care of your sister tonight," my mom said to Slade.

Slade was locked arm in arm with Avery and jabbed, "I got her, even though she made him wait."

"Oh no, it was no problem," Avery said, another reason why I liked him.

When we got to the tree lighting ceremony, Avery kissed Slade on the cheek and said,

"I got to go to the back. Mr. Mundy told me they want me to sing."

"Are you late?" Slade said, looking over at me.

"No, no, no, I'm cool. It was last minute, so they're just happy I can do it," he said, and I stuck out my tongue at my sister.

"Cool. I'm gonna find Charlotte, and we'll see you out here for ice skating."

"Ohhhh, I can't ice skate," he said to his girl.

"If I'm going to ice skate, you're going to do it. We'll fall down together," Slade said, looking at Avery all goo-goo eyed.

"That's wassup," he said, as he kissed her and dashed off.

"You really like him," I told my sister.

"Well, you look cute. But next time we got to go, don't let our sisters make you late. It's not cool."

"I'm sorry. I am nervous though."

"Don't be. You're adorable. This guy wanted to go out with you. I only met Charlotte's brother once, but he's a cutie. I just didn't know you were into the vanilla like that, girl. I like my coffee like mom."

She nudged me, and I nudged her back and said playfully, "With a little cream in it."

"Uh oh little sis!"

"Whatever, you're not that much older than me."

"Right, right, right."

"There he is! There he is!" I said, with more excitement than I knew I had as I saw Paris skating extremely comfortably. "I can't skate like that."

"Well, it looks like you'll have him to hold you up. Where's his sister?"

We both looked for her singing partner, and I froze when I spotted her. "I see Charlotte and umm . . ."

I didn't know how to describe it so I just pointed. Charlotte's lips were on another girl's lips. Slade was clearly shocked. Her eyebrows raised, and her mouth hung open.

"Oh my gosh! What is she doing? We got to end this. She can't be out in public kissing on a girl. I thought she was here with her date."

Popping her in the side, I said, "It looks like that is her date."

"Oh, nu uh. I am not having this," Slade said, wiggling her finger back and forth.

"You might own the record label, but you

don't own Charlotte. What's wrong with it anyway? What if she is with a girl?" I questioned.

"Uh!" Slade yelled out, heading straight over there to Charlotte.

I tried to stop her, but she headed straight to Charlotte. "What's all this? Who is this? I thought I was meeting your boyfriend."

"No, I told you I was coming with a date," Charlotte calmly told her, holding the taller brunette's hand as they swung them back and forth, obviously smitten with each other.

Slade got louder, working her neck and hips, trying to tell Charlotte what to do. Paris startled me when he came up behind me. I turned around.

"You look beautiful," he said.

"Thanks," I bashfully uttered as he leaned in and hugged me.

Slade said, "See that Charlotte, that's what's natural. What you're doing is crazy? I'm not going to be in a group with somebody who is . . ."

"What? You can't accept me? Then I don't need to be in a group with you. You're not my dictator, Slade. Come on, Jenna," Charlotte said to her date, and they were gone.

"Oh so you just gone walk off and leave?" Slade yelled from behind, but Charlotte didn't turn around.

It was getting ugly. I was so excited when the music started playing and Avery came on the stage. All Slade's yelling halted when she gave in to his beautiful voice.

I leaned over to my sister and said, "Now you see, that's what Christmas is about, loving on people, accepting them for who they are."

"Don't start, Yuri. We have an image to uphold. Charlotte's ticking me off. We're not staying because I don't want to run into her tail no more. You'll have to see this Paris guy another time." Slade walked towards the stage.

My sister and Charlotte were at an impasse. Paris and I were caught in the middle. I was a little disappointed that I wasn't going to get to hang out with him. However, I was so nervous about skating and having his arms wrapped around me that I was okay with having to postpone.

"At least let me buy you hot chocolate or something. You can come with me while I take my skates off," he said, overhearing that I had to go soon.

"I just don't know what my sister's problem is."

"Uh, my mom has the same problem, but Charlotte is her own girl, and Jenna's cool," Paris explained.

"They seem happy."

"I want to be happy with you. Can we talk about that?" he said, getting closer.

"Can we get some hot chocolate?" I laughed and said, before I was startled, looking up to find Ms. Pinky with another stand.

The lady was everywhere. Paris sat down on a nearby bench and took off his skates. I walked to the dessert stand. She dropped two cookies, picked them up, blew them off and put them back inside a plastic bag to sell. I was stunned.

"I know you're not going to sell those," I yelled out.

Ms. Pinky either didn't see me or ignored me. She went around back, completely ignoring me. The lady was crazy, and so was Slade. And maybe so was I, more ready to leave a date than try and enjoy one. What a crazy night.

***

"Girls, it's time to go," my mother yelled out the next evening when we had to accompany my parents to the Christmas party.

As the mayor-elect, my dad was the special guest, and he was on program to give a speech. None of us wanted to go. The designer Shelby was working with was having a Christmas party. Shelby and Ansli wanted to go to that. Avery was preforming at another party, and Slade wanted to accompany him. Sloan wanted to be at a Marks High School basketball game. Reese was playing, and she wanted to see him. I too had other plans I could have entertained. Paris called earlier, and his parents were going to take us to dinner. My parents weren't budging. They knew if they let one of us go our own way, all of us would have to be let off the hook.

"The limousine is here, girls. Your dad is not going to wait," my mom called out.

"I'm down. It's the other four," Slade said as she passed my door.

"I'm out too," I said, remembering what she told me yesterday about not letting my sisters make me late.

I mean sometimes there just wasn't that much primping in the world. Shelby and Ansli had no excuse in my opinion because the two of them shared a bathroom. Slade, Sloan, and I had to share one bathroom. Yet when Sloan came down, it was the two older sisters who were taking the longest. When we got in the car, my mom was fussing at our tardiness, but I noticed my dad was so quiet. None of us had really seen him much the last week, he'd been so busy. The others didn't know what I knew about some of Dad's health issues.

I still wanted to ask him, "So did you get to the doctor? What did the doctor say? Do you need some medicine? Have you taken the proper rest? Talk to me." But he could barely hold his head up. He was sweating. It was cold. In the bar of the limousine there were bottles of water. I took one, opened it, and drank a little.

"Anybody else want some?" I said, hoping my dad would say yes.

When he didn't, I just handed him a bottle. He refused it and handed it back to me. I was so frustrated.

As soon as we got to the Christmas party, my dad perked up. I could not explain it, but it was like he knew when to shine. He was waving, shaking hands, and doing everything a politician should.

I knew we were big time when we got announced on the loud speaker, "Mayor-Elect Stanley Sharp and his family!"

People stopped in the ballroom and just started clapping. I knew I was going to have to get used to the attention. However, I just wished people wouldn't make us into such a big deal.

"Yuri, there you are!" Ms. Pinky squealed coming out of nowhere.

I could have thrown up. What was she doing at the mayor's party? Why did I have to know her? I wanted to choke her for selling dirty cookies.

She continued, “Hello, dear! Your dad’s gone up ahead, darn! But I’d love to meet your mother.”

“My mom’s way up ahead too,” I told her.

“Well honey what good is it going to do me to work with you if I’m not going to get the perks in public? If all my friends around here see me talking to the first family-elect, my stocks stay up.”

“What are you doing here anyway, Ms. Pinky?”

“I’m a vendor for the city.”

“You?”

“Yeah, I cater a lot of the parties. I’m not catering tonight but . . . oh quit talking and take me up there to your mom.”

“I don’t even see them anymore. I have to introduce you to them later.”

“Whatever!” Ms. Pinky said as she briskly walked away, heading to cozy up to someone across the way that she deemed important.

“That lady is a little snooty,” Sloan said.

“Yeah, you only know the half of it.”

“Watch your back with her.”

"I don't want to work for her," I said, noticing she had sashayed on up to my parents on her own.

I realized she was not going to let me stand in the way of her own personal agenda. Sloan was dead on. Ms. Pinky had to be watched.

Finally, we got to our table. The table sat eight. There were seven of us in my family, so we had one extra seat. I didn't even want to stay there when Ms. Pinky walked over with my parents.

My mom said, "Yuri, look who's going to join us. Girls change up the seats so that Ms. Pinky can sit beside Yuri."

I looked at Sloan like "don't you dare move," but my sis had no choice. There I was, having to sit beside the phoniest woman in the city of Charlotte. She talked our ears off throughout dinner. I was so happy when it was my dad's time to give his speech.

My dad took the mic and said, "I love this time of year, the holiday season, so merry and bright. It makes me think of the future of this great city. The sun is shining our way,

Charlottians, and I am just honored to know our current mayor has done a great job. And I am honored and humbled that you all have given me a chance to pick up where he . . . where he . . ."

My dad started stuttering. Then he was shaking, and the next thing you know, he was flat on the ground. My mom stood in horror. My sisters were in shock. The crowd was in awe. I was miserable. Clearly, he hadn't gone to the doctor. Surely, I shouldn't have kept what I had known about his health to myself. As all of us rushed to the stage, I stopped dead in my tracks. I hated that I let my dad talk me into keeping his ill health a secret. I felt worse than horrible wondering why did I yield?

CHAPTER FIVE
YOU

"Get my girls out of here!" my mom screamed out, seeing the five of us in a panic. "Stanley is going to be fine. I just know it, but they need to go. Someone get them out of here now."

All of us were utter basket cases as we watched our unresponsive father lie helpless. None of us wanted to move or go anywhere, but my mom was adamant. Though she was trying to be positive, she didn't want us seeing our father in this dire situation.

Ms. Pinky and the current mayor's wife escorted us out of the room. We couldn't leave behind the mayhem. Many people were trying to figure out what was wrong with my father. Doctors who were in attendance had come up on stage. The five of us knew nothing except we were being shoved into a limo.

"Please take them home, sir," the mayor's wife said to our limo driver.

But as soon as she stepped away, Shelby said, "No, no, no!. We're not going anywhere. They can get us out of the room, but they can't make us leave. Please wait a second."

Ansli and Sloan were crying. Shelby and Slade were angry. I was still in shock. And when we heard an ambulance, we knew that wasn't a good sign. Our father needed emergency attention. This was serious. It felt like hours went by as we sat and waited for the ambulance to get to moving.

After ten minutes, the limousine driver let down the window and asked, "Are you ladies ready to go now?"

Shelby yelled, "No, did we say we were ready? Shucks! We're following the ambulance to the hospital when it leaves out. That's where we're going, and that's when we're moving."

"But I have strict orders to take you to your residence," he said, recalling the mayor's wife's direction.

Shelby leaned to the window. "Man, can you hear? Those plans have been amended, and we have money if we need to pay you more."

"No, no, it's covered. I just didn't know. I'm sorry," he said in a calming voice, realizing she was going to tear him to pieces if he didn't concede.

"Yeah, you don't have to bite off the man's head," I said to Shelby, wanting my sister to calm down. It was freaking me out that she was so upset.

"Don't tell me how to respond, Yuri. Don't tell me how to feel," Shelby screamed.

"You don't have to jump on Yuri!" Sloan yelled back at her.

I shouted, "No, it's fine, Sloan. I can take whatever she's dishing out. This is a lot. This is hard on all of us."

"Yeah, we need to stick together," Ansli said, helping me bring peace to the growing chaos.

"We're family. Let's act like one."

"If Dad is dead, what kind of family do we have?" Slade blurted out, quieting us all.

We were all way too stressed. Slade had a good point. If our dad was gone, we'd never be the same. It was taking the emergency crew an awful long time. Did that mean he was already gone? The waiting was torture.

Thankfully about five minutes later, the ambulance took off. Our mother had to be inside of it because we never saw her. Slade started praying. We grabbed on one another's hands, bowed our heads, and joined her. When all their eyes were closed, I opened mine. I looked up out at the sky and just wished I could go back in time. If so, I would have told my mother what I witnessed with my dad, and then maybe all of this could have been avoided. My heart was heavy as I knew this was all my fault.

We couldn't go as fast as the ambulance. So when we got to the hospital, the ambulance had already unloaded him. The five of us got out of the limo quicker than we'd ever gotten out of any vehicle.

Shelby rushed over to the desk, trying to find our mother. The four of us were circled together hoping for great news. Shelby didn't look pleased when she came back over to brief us.

"I think she's back there with him or something. Nobody is telling me anything. I don't know what's going on with our dad." She went and sank on a nearby couch.

"If he was dead, we'd know," Slade said, going over to Shelby to keep her uplifted.

"Yeah right, we'd know," Sloan looked at Ansli and me and voiced hopefully.

Just then the mayor and his wife rushed into the emergency waiting room. He asked, "Have you girls heard anything?"

We all shook our heads. I saw his wife squinting, probably wondering why we defied her orders. I smiled her way hoping she'd not ask and just give us grace.

The mayor said, "Okay, I'm going to try and find some answers. Stay here with my wife. He's going to be okay."

"So he wasn't dead on the scene?" Slade asked, sniffing.

"No, he still wasn't responding, but he was with us," the mayor said. "And ladies don't worry, Charlotte has some of the finest physicians in this great hospital."

The mayor was going on and on and on. I wanted to cut him off. We didn't even need a political speech. We knew Charlotte was great, but at this moment we needed to know that our father was okay. And if he couldn't tell us that, then he didn't need to tell us anything.

"I thought you girls were going to go home?" his wife asked us once the mayor walked away to go find answers.

"If it was your dad, could you go home?" Shelby stood and said to her.

"Point taken," his wife said. "I just wanted to honor your mother's wishes. I do, however, understand. I surely would have come here too."

We were all on edge. Seeing my sisters going through was eating me up even more. I needed space. I walked over to a corner to breathe.

Sloan followed. "What's wrong?"

"Same thing that's wrong with everybody," I

said to her, unable to look her way. "I'm worried about Dad."

"No, no, no, I know you. Something else is going on. It's like you're carrying the weight of all this."

When she said that, I busted out crying. "That's because it's my fault."

She tried to grab my hand. "What are you talking about?"

I stepped back and shared, "I knew Dad was sick."

Then she stepped back and looked at me wanting an explanation. I had to tell all at that point. Sloan wouldn't let me if I decided to keep quiet now.

Tired of keeping what I kept a secret any longer, I shared, "I was with him a couple times, and he was faint and dizzy. He almost passed out, but he didn't, and he made me promise not to say anything but . . ."

Rolling her eyes, she cut me off and asked, "Wait, you knew he wasn't a hundred percent? You knew he was ill, and you didn't tell?"

She was so loud. My sister and best friend's

eyes turned red, and her temples were bulging out. I had never seen someone so angry and so mad at me.

"Why would you not say anything? Why would you keep this to yourself? Why would you at least not tell me?"

"Because he made me promise!" I yelled back. "That's what I was trying to tell you."

"So what? That's supposed to make it better that you betrayed us! Now he's in there fighting for his life! He might even be gone, and you knew and you didn't say anything!"

Feeling like she was squeezing my heart in her hand, I uttered, "But I couldn't . . ."

Cutting me off again, she said, "What? You want our dad to be dead like your dad is? Is that what this is?"

At that point, she had said words that she couldn't take back. She looked me dead in my eyes and said, "I hate you."

Hearing her harsh words, I rushed out of the room, feeling forever broken. Even if my dad was okay, my relationship with my best friend could never be mended again. I sat alone and cried and cried and cried and cried, wanting my life to be better, but knowing it couldn't be. Too much I had left unsaid, and I ruined my family.

***

"Oh my gosh, Yuri, there you are! Where is Slade?" Charlotte said to me.

Quickly, I started wiping my tears. I didn't want her to see me so devastated. I was so choked up that I could barely get myself together. Charlotte draped her arms around me.

"It's going to be okay. Let it all out. I understand," she said.

"It's not going to be okay. You don't understand," I whimpered.

"You've got to believe that your dad is going to be okay. You've got to stay positive. Why aren't y'all all together? Where are your sisters?" Charlotte said to me as she looked around for the other Sharp girls.

I couldn't tell her why I was all alone. She'd hate me if she knew that had I opened my mouth, my dad might not be in this situation. I just cried harder until I saw Slade with Charlotte's brother, Paris, coming around the corner.

"I found her, Charlotte," Paris called out to his sister.

As they approached us, I completely turned my back to all three of them. I'm sure Sloan had told everyone what I had done. I didn't want to hear Slade go off on me too. I was beating myself up enough anyway. If I could trade places with my dad lying in the hospital bed, I would have. Being me wasn't working out.

"Your brother told me you were looking for me. You didn't have to come," I heard Slade say to Charlotte.

Charlotte said, "Of course I did. When my dad got home all in a panic about what he witnessed at the mayor's ball, I had to be here for you. On the news it said which hospital your dad was in, so we came for support. Forget our beef. I'm here for you guys."

The last time the two of them were together, there was much tension because Slade didn't approve of Charlotte's relationship. Thankfully, they threw all that out the window. My tough sister Slade didn't break down like me, but she was talking to her girlfriend and singing partner. Slade was appreciative for her support.

Slade articulated, "I can't believe I judged you, Charlotte. Life is so fragile. You're here and fine one second, and then the next, you're not. I thought I knew everything. I just want our group to have a chance, but I can't rule your life."

"I know, I know. I've been thinking about what you said, and can see how it would have freaked you out. I probably should have told you. But none of that is important right now. I just came to support you."

As soon as I started to walk forward, Slade called my name. "You, don't you dare go anywhere."

The hasty tone she used made me run far away from her, straight out the doors of the hospital. I only hated that I didn't have a car so that I could get in it and drive even further away. But there I stood out of breath at the corner of the hospital and a drug store.

"So you done running?" I heard Paris say.

I turned around. "Just go back. Leave me alone."

"You need somebody to talk to, Yuri. It's dark out here. You got on a dark dress. You look gorgeous by the way, but people can't even see you. Come on back in. It can't be that bad."

Huffing I said, "You don't know, okay."

He touched my shoulders and said, "I got a pretty good idea of what you're carrying around. Remember I was with you the other day when your dad was a little woozy."

"Yeah, but what you don't know is that he had another incident. When we left the concert, he had a charity event, and he passed out there too. I wanted to tell my mom. I wanted to tell my sisters. I wanted to say something, but he told me not to. He made me promise."

"I get that. So why are you beating yourself up about it?"

"Because I shouldn't have promised. It's my dad's health, and obviously I didn't realize it was as serious as it was. I guess I told Sloan, thinking she'd take the weight off, understand, and make me feel better. We all know how stubborn my dad can be. Instead, she went off on me. I guess I was just living in la la land any way thinking

I'm not to blame for all this. I did this."

"Your father is an adult. He is the mayor-elect for goodness sake. Come on now, he knew what he was doing. You're not responsible for his actions."

"But I'm responsible for mine," I said, looking up to the sky and wishing I was a star so I could disappear and illuminate brightness instead of the darkness I felt was clouding my family.

"Can I hold you?" he asked taking me off guard.

I just looked at him. Now wasn't a time for me to get romantic. My world had fallen apart. My father was clinging on for his life. He had to know I wanted distance. Not caring what I wanted, he gave me what I needed. He held me and wouldn't let go. I let out the tears I hadn't finish crying with his sister on his shoulder.

"We're young, Yuri. We're not always going to make the right choices, but as long as your motives are pure and you're trying your best, it will work out."

"Even this?" I said to him.

"Even this," he answered, giving me the comfort in his words that I needed.

***

"Come on, let's go back over there with your sisters," Paris said. "I'm sure that they're not mad."

"I just told you Sloan was. In my house, it's always a chain reaction. So if she's mad, everybody else is too."

"Do you want to be afraid to face your sisters all your life? Okay, I get that you're the baby. I'm the baby in my household too. And I've got an older brother, so I get the whole sibling thing, but there's got to come a point when you're tired of being pushed around. You didn't do anything. And if you won't say nothing, then I'll stand up to whichever one of your sisters who's got a problem with you about it," Paris defended, ready to have my back.

"You're sweet," I said, smiling and starting to feel better. "Okay, how hard can it be?"

But as soon as I started walking around the corner, Sloan saw me and said, "How dare you show your face back over here? We're waiting to hear what's going on with Dad, and you knew and didn't even say anything."

"You too?" Shelby rushed over to me and said. I guess our oldest sister had been with our dad a couple of times too and saw he was less than stable. "I've been toiling so much, feeling bad about keeping all this a secret and you saw him weak too?"

I nodded. We just embraced. I was just waiting for Sloan to go off on Shelby, thinking she wouldn't, but she did.

"This is crazy! Both of y'all think it's okay, happy that the other was keeping this a secret too. We could have done something. We could have got him to the hospital before he ended up in the hospital, practically unable to come out. Both of you are idiots."

"Why you thinking so negative?" Ansli asked her. "You see them beating themselves up about it."

Sloan scoffed, "Whatever. Just like I told your sister, you know what . . . forget it."

"No, what," Ansli got in Sloan's face and

said. “What’d you tell Yuri? What do you, mean ‘my sister?’ We really going to do this? This is really going to be us against you guys?”

“No, we’re *not* going to do that!” Shelby said while frowning at Sloan.

Everybody was looking at me wondering what Sloan said? They all figured it was a repulsive statement. It absolutely was. I was heartbroken. I was hardly able to shake the fact that she accused me of wanting our parents to be dead like my birth parents were. I couldn’t even repeat that. I didn’t even want to put more hate out in the air that could never be taken back, so I just looked away.

“But what you accused me of . . .” I said to Sloan under my breath, “. . . would that be the same for Shelby? We were just trying to honor Dad’s wishes, keep what he had going on in the inside to ourselves. I wasn’t trying to hurt him, and I certainly didn’t think he would end up in the hospital. If he doesn’t come out, I’ll never be able to forgive myself. Regardless of if anybody else knew, I still feel horrible that I didn’t tell.”

“That’s how I feel too,” Shelby said as she

placed her arm around my shoulder.

Ansli locked in on my other arm. "But he's going to be okay. He is."

"Y'all hope so," I said to my two big sisters.

"Sloan, I hear you talking a bunch of junk, but you don't know what you would have done if Dad asked you to keep the secret." Shelby laid into her.

"Just because you make stupid decisions doesn't mean I would too," Sloan yelled back. "Shelby, your actions may have killed Dad."

Shelby pushed Sloan. "You witch."

We were in the emergency room waiting area, and my sisters were acting like we were young again, fussing in our own backyard. The police guards rushed over. So did Slade and Charlotte. But the argument only intensified.

When my mom rushed out, she yelled, "What is going on out here? Girls!"

We all calmed down, and we rushed over to her.

"Sorry, Mom!" Shelby yelled out.

"Yeah, I'm sorry. How's Dad?" Sloan asked.

"He's going to be fine," she finally said.

Big sighs of relief flooded our faces. The grimness faded. Those were the words we'd been waiting to hear.

"He's going to be okay?" I asked again, tears flowing, anticipating the answer staying the same.

"Yes, baby, he's going to be okay," my mom said as she hugged me.

"I'm so sorry. I knew something was wrong with him. He passed out a couple times on me, and I, I should have said something," I admitted, knowing my mom was going to hate me for keeping this information.

"Me too, Mom," Shelby said, surprising me as she also admitted she knew Dad wasn't totally well.

Sloan stepped to my mom, wanting her to get on us. "Yes, they should have said something! That's why we're arguing. Dad wouldn't have been in here if they would have said something!"

My mom took Sloan's hand. "Well, I knew he wasn't well too. Your dad has diabetes. He hasn't been taking good care of himself, so I'm just as much to blame as anybody is. And the last thing he'd want any of us to do is to blame ourselves. He is a stubborn mule who, from now on, won't be taking any of this lightly."

Sloan was flabbergasted. I was astonished too. Paris winked my way, letting me know I was cool to keep quiet. Shelby nodded, getting the fact that it was hard for a lot of us to go against my dad. I could tell Sloan felt bad she was so hard on me. I still felt I deserved it, but the best part was my dad was okay. Now I needed to be educated about his condition.

"Diabetes?" I pondered.

My mom said, "Yes baby. We'll be pushing your dad, but we didn't do this too him. I don't want any of you girls to fret. But now we know we just need to look after him. But what happened to him tonight was not on me or you."

CHAPTER SIX
YUMMY

I was so happy there was only one week of school left before the Christmas break. I so needed to get away from so much, but I realized I was blessed. We had finally gotten home from the hospital, and although I couldn't sleep, I was certainly more at ease knowing my dad was downstairs resting.

There was a knock on my door, and then it opened. "It's me, Sloan. You up?"

Inside there was a serious battle going on within me. I wanted to tell her, no! Get the heck out, jerk! But I knew we needed to talk. And if she had felt some type of way that she couldn't sleep, obviously she'd realized she'd crossed the line. Maybe resolving it now was a good thing.

"Yeah, I'm up," she came over and sat on my bed. Usually she never needed an invitation for such an action, but cutting the fool and acting crazy with me as she had, I said, "Excuse you?"

"This is hard, Yuri. I don't know what came over me," Sloan said.

"You made it pretty clear that you don't really think I'm your sister."

"But you know that's not true."

Shaking my head, I said, "Actions speak louder than words, Sloan. I was already beating myself up, and you came and made it way worse. I don't know if you trying to pay me back for everything that happened last month. I mean, I don't know."

"Maybe internally I was acting out a little because of that. I thought you should have believed me when I said I didn't take the picture of myself. I certainly didn't send a naked picture to Reese."

"I get that, and I apologize, but please don't forget I was also the one that helped you find out what really happened. I never said anything to make you feel like you weren't related. To say I wanted your parents dead like mine, I just don't get that. Obviously it's bothering me because I can't even sleep."

"Well, it's bothering me too. That's why I'm in here."

"I see that, but how do we get past such harsh words?"

"You've always been the bigger person, Yuri. You've always had a big heart. I guess I came in here to ask you to find some way to forgive me. Just the thought of losing my father—*our* father . . ." she said, correcting her own words, ". . . is scary. Thinking on it, you, Shelby, and Mom, made a good point. If Dad asked me to keep his secret, I probably would have done the same thing."

I was glad she was coming around, but I still had bigger issues with what she'd said. "Even though you were mad at me, how could you take it to the level you did? You hurt me, Sloan."

"I was stupid to say that mean stuff. I thought I learned something last month that I don't know it all, you know? But, Yuri, we're about to turn sixteen. We're both growing. We're both changing, and I'm learning I'm not perfect. I know you hate me," Sloan uttered, looking sad.

"I love you, Sloan," I let slip from the depths of my soul.

"You still do?" she said, getting a little emotional. "Because I love you too. You're my best friend, and I need some grace." We hugged.

"Well you will be proud of me on this, Yuri. I know the baking contest is coming up tomorrow, and I got a ton of people who're ready to taste your cupcakes and vote for you."

"That's right, that thing is tomorrow. Why can't it just be Christmas break already?" I squealed, placing the covers over my head.

Sloan pulled the covers back. "What's wrong with you? You love baking, and how's it going with Ms. Pinky, anyway? It was too cool to see Paris all in your corner at the hospital." I just smiled.

"Get some rest," she said as she kissed me on my cheek and tucked me in the bed.

She used to love doing that when we were little. We're just a couple days apart, but she liked pretending like she was the big, big sister. Now that that was settled, I went to sleep with ease. Forgiveness is a great thing. Even when you don't think you have it in your heart to be able to forgive, once you try—I mean really want to mend the relationship—love makes it easy.

Nine hours later it was twelve o'clock in the afternoon, and I was in the cafeteria with my red velvet cupcakes. My sisters had come through. My line was the longest. There were six contestants. We each had to bake one hundred cupcakes and whosever were gone first, based on word of mouth or by marketing, was the contest winner. As soon as Ms. Newton said go, my cupcakes were gone first. Everybody was talking about how delicious they were. I won. It felt good being victorious in something I loved. As soon as I felt on top of the world, I spotted Logan looking dejected. Though I was out of the hundred cupcakes I brought, I had two extras that I was going to eat for myself. I took them both and went over to her.

"Here, you want one?" I said, handing one to her.

She shook her head. "Please don't tempt me. I come to school, and I can't really eat anything, and I certainly don't need any cupcakes. Look at me; I'm a slob."

"You're beautiful," I said to her. "What's wrong with a few curves here and there?" I said, trying to lighten the mood.

"I'm just tired of getting picked on. I'm tired of my own battle. I hate my whole life."

I scooted my chair closer to her and leaned in and said, "Logan, I'm worried about you. Your life is valuable, but you gotta know that."

"I'm trying to believe that. You being nice to me has meant a lot. But sometimes I just can't see any reason to go on."

My heart was so heavy at that moment. "Logan, you have so much to live for."

"I'm trying to believe you, but who am I?"

I placed my hand on her shoulder and said,

"You're a girl who deserves a chance in this life. A chance to reach your hopes and dreams. A chance to achieve anything. A chance at happiness. I'm working on my own weaknesses. You can do the same. Just don't give up on you. You've still got so much to do."

"Just you taking the time to say that to me, Yuri, gives me hope. I am worthy of living. Thank you so much."

***

"There you are," Rhonda said as I entered Ms. Pinky's for another lesson.

I was going to have to get a backbone. My parents needed to understand this lady had nothing to teach me, but because I didn't want to upset my dad while he was recuperating or bother my mom while she was into her case, I followed instructions.

My sister Slade dropped me off. I so wish Ansli was off punishment and driving again. I missed our talks. Unfortunately, back in September she skipped school with the car and lost her privileges until further notice, and my parents hadn't given her notice that she could start driving again.

"Is she here?" I said to Rhonda.

Rhonda pointed her head towards the back. "She wanted to show you how to make some crust, but she needed to get it in the oven an hour ago, and you weren't around, so she's a little upset. She wants to be able to teach you some things, but she's just not trying to go above and beyond so you better let her know you're here."

I huffed. But before I could step to the back, she stepped to the front. Her mean face showed she detested me.

Frowning she huffed, "I thought I heard someone—you can't call? I didn't know if you were going to stop coming or what. I mean, I'm not here to hold your hand, and while I'm not paying you, I could have other people working with me because I do need extra hands."

I thought, *You just want free labor. Me doing your work so that you won't have to do it yourself.* Before she got a chance to fuss at me anymore, customers came in, which was exciting. Though I looked at the pretty treats, in my mind I thought,

Don't eat them! Don't want one! Something's wrong! Maybe she made it with outdated ingredients; maybe she dropped it on the floor, which was hard to accept because, again, everything really looked delicious. Who knows what else could be wrong with her goodies? More than likely something was.

A lady pulling a little girl who looked weak said, "I need to speak to Ms. Pinky."

She was bent down on the floor getting muffins out of a box. Ms. Pinky stood up after she put the new treats in the display. "Yes, what do you need from me? What do you want?"

Both Rhonda and I looked at her like, why would you talk to your customer that way?

Ms. Pinky continued even harsher. "You're the same lady who called me earlier, right? I can tell by your voice. Now you got your pitiful little child in here, and you want to make me feel bad. I did not make your baby sick."

"Well, I need to know what you put in your cookies when we were at the ice skating rink. And this isn't even my same daughter. My other baby's at home even more ill. She's allergic to a lot, and I specifically asked you if you had peanut oil."

Ms. Pinky rudely stated, "No, I don't put peanut oil in my cookies. Read my lips, I did not make your baby sick. Whatever's going on—she probably got into something at home when you weren't watching."

The mom continued, "Because my children are allergic to things, I watch them all the time. It's something about her not feeling well from your food that's just got me so stressed because it's something new. She can't hold anything down. It's like a stomach virus, like it was food poisoning or something, and I'm not—"

"Are you saying that I've been trying to make people sick? Get out of my store! Get out of my store!" Ms. Pinky continued to yell.

"No, this is about my child!" the lady stood there and said.

If the one who was with her wasn't the one who was really sick, I'd hate to see the sicker one because the one who was with her looked so limp and helpless.

"She had a bite of her sister's cookie, but she

didn't eat the whole thing, and now this one is sick. I'm not trying to sue you or close you down or anything, but I just need to know so I can help my child."

"You don't wanna leave? Oh, I'm gonna call the cops." Ms. Pinky said as she went to pick up the phone, but the lady didn't move.

"Great, that's what you need to do. You know what? I'm not gonna make your job easier for you. You don't wanna call them because you've done something wrong. I will be back. If something happens to my daughter . . ."

"What? What?" Ms. Pinky said without an ounce of empathy.

When the lady left, Ms. Pinky started screaming. She was pacing back and forth behind the counter. She took one of her root beer mugs and tossed it clear across the store, shattering it into pieces.

"I'm gonna mess up my pies fooling with this lady! I didn't do anything to her daughter. Clean that up, Yuri! And Rhonda come and help me with this!" Ms. Pinky said, walking to the back.

When I got the broom, I immediately started sweeping up the glass and bent down with the dust pail to pick it up, and in a flash, the memory of a couple cupcakes falling to the ground at the ice skating rink immediately came to mind. Maybe that little girl had eaten one of them. I had told Ms. Pinky she needed to throw them out, but she refused. I was with Paris then, and I was so into wanting to say goodbye to him that I never made sure that the items were discarded. Maybe I needed to call the police. Maybe I needed to run after that mother. Maybe I needed to tell my mom. After all, she was working on a case dealing with food.

When the door opened, I was stunned to see Paris. I dashed over to him and said, "You gotta help me figure this out."

"Yeah, sure anything. What's going on? Your dad okay? Is it Onyx?"

"Nothing about the gang today. My father is resting. It's your aunt."

His warmth faded. "I don't follow."

"It's everything about her and this place. It looks like she's the world's best pastry chef, but that's not the case. When we were at the skating rink, I saw her with my own eyes cut corners."

"Are you accusing my aunt of doing something illegal with her food?" he asked as he backed up, clearly insulted.

I explained, "Yes, I am, and I wouldn't say it if I didn't have proof. She uses spoiled ingredients. Items that she doesn't sell she keeps for days, and she only puts new frosting on them and then sticks them in the microwave so people will think they're fresh. And she dropped some items on the floor and sold them to people, and a little girl is sick. Maybe deathly ill."

"Okay, you're exaggerating, Yuri. I know you felt all bad that you didn't help your dad before something drastic happened, but you don't have to try and go overboard in this instance and ruin my aunt."

"I would never!"

"You clearly are. I just thought you were bigger and better than what you're showing me now."

"I know she's your aunt, but I surely thought you cared about right and wrong." I handed him the broom, took the dustpan, and dumped the whole thing in the trash. I grabbed my coat and purse and left out, heading down the street to the local bookstore to pass my hour before Slade came back to pick me up. Regardless of what Paris thought, something was going to have to be done. This was a yucky situation.

***

Sipping on hot cocoa in the bookstore, I texted Slade, "Long story, not at the dessert shop. Pick me up at the bookstore. Please hurry. My life is falling apart."

After I hit send, I wanted to take back the message, or at least take back the last part.

Slade quickly called me back and said, "I know you didn't get fired from a volunteer job? Charlotte told me her brother works there. Were you all over him instead of taking care of your responsibilities and the lady let you go?"

Sighing I said, "No, sis, could you just hurry up please? That's not what happened."

"I'm not the one coming to pick you up. Ansli is."

"So why you got me going into all of this?"

"You the one who texted me! Charlotte and I are practicing for a few gigs, so please don't blow things with her family."

"You're talking to me about blowing up on somebody?"

"All that is behind us now, Yuri."

"Okay, but let me call Ansli."

"I'm just sayin' if you need to apologize, you need to apologize."

I hated that Slade was so into making her world right that she didn't really listen to those around her, just like with Charlotte. She cared more about their image than Charlotte's needs, and if she'd listened to me here, or at least give me a chance to explain, she would understand why I wanted to be far away from Ms. Pinky's facility.

I actually needed to talk to Ansli, anyway. Her personality was more like mine than anyone else's in our home. I was certain it was because we were biological sisters. Maybe I needed to bond more with her, get her to help me understand how she maneuvers in such a, sometimes, volatile home. I used to think it was really cute that Shelby, Slade, and Sloan were so fiery. Now I was getting a little agitated, and I wanted to get those feelings under control before they became a bad issue. Fifteen minutes after I texted, Ansli was out front of the bookstore. I knew she loved white, hot chocolate with extra whipped cream, so I got her a cup before heading outside.

"I know that's not what I think it is," she said.

I nodded, handing it to her. "Yum, yum before I even tasted it. I love you girl! Why'd you bring me a cup? What's going on? You don't have to bribe your sister if you want to talk to your sister. You know that?"

"I just wanted to try to do something nice for you, that's all."

"Thank you!" Her tongue was nothing like mine. It took me a while before I could drink a hot liquid, but she turned that cup up like nothing. "Delicious! You made my world right. How can I do the same for yours?"

"I used to wish I was stronger, you know like our sisters. I've been asserting myself more lately, and it's been getting me into trouble. I guess I've learned it's not so bad to stay the Yuri that I am, but even that person is evolving because nobody's pushing me up to stand up more for myself or more for others. I don't know, I can't explain it. I feel so confused."

"I don't tell you often enough, but you are the best person I know," Ansli said to me. "You see the good in everybody and everything more than the rest of us. You make everything that's wrong, right. And you're much stronger than you think you are. You might be quiet and not loud and demanding with your delivery, but you're equally as passionate. You always have been. And I know you don't remember, and I'm not trying to make you sad or anything, but we do have an angel up there watching over us, and you remind me so much of our biological mom."

"I do?" I said to her.

"You are right. You don't need to change you, Yuri. Just keep growing, learning from your mistakes, and understanding what you will and won't accept. But I saw you during Slade's concert, and for the first time ever, I saw a side of you that scared me a little bit. Well, that and when you had Onyx ready to fight you of all of us. You're the last person I would think a gang would wanna get on, but whatever."

"I know, right?" I said to her. "What did you notice at the concert?"

Then before she said anything, I could remember back. I knew what it was. I'd allowed the green-eyed monster to show its ugly head.

"You've always been one who has been happy for other people," Ansli explained. "Don't change that. What's going on with this Ms. Pinky lady? I heard about you and Charlotte's brother."

"We won't ever be talking again," I said defiantly.

"Okay, so you like him," Ansli teased.

"No, I don't. I mean how can you take up for someone who's doing wrong?"

"You can't, but there's always two sides to every story, and sometimes people have to find out things for themselves for them to come around. So don't be too hard on him, and if there's something serious going on with Ms. Pinky, tell

Dad. When I tried to take some things into my own hands, with all that stuff that was going on with some of those homeless people, it didn't work out until I got Dad involved."

"How's he feeling?" I asked when we pulled up at the house.

"Go check in on him. I had some time with him earlier."

"So is he not doing well?"

"I didn't say that, Yuri. He's fine and on the strictest diet. He's sad because the sweets are gone."

"I can make him a treat. I've been thinking about this for my friend, Logan. She can't eat a lot of sweets either, and desserts are so sugary sometimes, but they don't always have to be."

"Well, go hook them up. You'll really make him smile."

***

An hour later, I was walking into my parents' bedroom.

"Ooh, what do you have here?" he said

already sitting up. "I hope everybody told you I can't have that though."

"You can eat this one, Dad. No sugars anywhere."

"Then I don't wanna eat that one. It looks good, but it won't taste worth anything."

"Trust me," I said to him.

"Alright. Your mom told me you've been a little upset. Beating yourself up because you didn't divulge what you witnessed earlier with me and my health."

"Yeah, Dad, you scared me."

"I apologize for putting you in such a tough position. But I love you with all my heart, and I am okay. I'm just going to have to watch what I eat."

"Well, take this. Everybody deserves a treat and this one is the healthy kind because you know all the Sharp girls are ready to comply. Mom included."

"Oh, I know. Everybody's letting me have it. But what's going on with you?"

"Dad, I don't wanna work for Ms. Pinky anymore."

"Why not, baby girl?"

I explained everything to my father. All I witnessed, all that Rhonda told me, and all my fears of what would happen if nothing was done.

"Wow. You'll never know what shortcuts people take," he said. "Look, you don't worry about this, nor will you have to go back unless I need you to go with me. We're going to take it over from here."

"You will, Daddy?"

"Yeah, and Dr. Garner also called me about his concerns with this gang threatening you. What's up with that?"

"I stood up for the right person at the wrong time, but it's okay. I don't think they're bothering me anymore."

"Well, we're looking into all of that too, but you stay far away from them."

"Yes, sir. You don't have to worry."

He was squinting looking at my cupcake, like no way could something healthy taste good.

"Eat it. Taste it, Dad!"

He bit into it, and the natural sweetness made it yummy.

CHAPTER SEVEN

YULETIDE

Sometimes to get things perfect you've got to deal with the tough stuff. But the reason situations are tough is because most people don't want to deal with it. That's when people need to be encouraged and empowered to stand up and take appropriate action. Well, that's what the school was doing. SGA and PTSA partnered with administration to put on a rally to address bullying. In the last few days alone, not only were people getting beat up physically, but the gang was stealing and also threatening to shoot up the school. Many were terrified.

Logan and I were asked to share our story. The gym was full. You would have thought it was somebody's graduation day with the way the place was packed as parents and community folks showed up in support. I was so nervous. After all, I wasn't as great a speaker as my sisters. However, I tried to shake it off because I did have something to say on the subject. Once Reese, the PTSA student leader, introduced me, I got the nerve to head to the podium and speak up.

"No one should be afraid to come to school. It's a place where you're supposed to come to get a great education, not worry about being the victim of violence. I got involved in an incident, and didn't feel like I could sit there and not say something. I know now that you can't always speak up alone. I guess that's why we're having this forum. A lot is going on, and it's not even completely comfortable for me to get up now, but if we don't stand up and fight those who are trying to destroy us, then they're taking away what matters most, and that's our future. Without a future we have no life. So if you know something about someone getting bullied, if you've been bullied yourself, if you're bulling somebody, just take time to think about what you're doing to make this place better. That's all I have to say." I let out a sigh and turned to head back to my seat.

Reese was mouthing something to me. I couldn't make out what he was saying. I squinted. He repeated himself much louder, and I got it.

"Oh, I'm supposed to introduce my friend Logan. Give her a hand," I said.

Nobody clapped. They just sort of looked at me like I was silly. But as long as they heard what we had to say, the applause didn't matter.

Logan came up to the podium, and I tried to go sit down. She grabbed my hand, and she started crying. Not boo-hoo crying, but steady tears streamed down her face. It didn't matter if you were close to or far away from her, you could tell there was some serious emotion being let out. It's like the whole gym just changed. Before she even spoke a word, her tears united us.

Finally, she got herself together, and she said, "If it wasn't for this girl here, I probably would be dead. She stood up for me when no one would. She's given me hope when I had none, and she's helped me learn that I am somebody special. Yeah, my parents have been telling me that for years in their own crazy way—my dad is a little rough around the edges. However, I didn't understand it as much as I did when she said it. Because as y'all can tell, I'm a big, big girl. I eat too many sweets, and I have for far too long. I'm also a diabetic. Because of my choices, my life is in danger. I was living with all of that. I was dealing with all of that, but there were some cruel people who wouldn't leave me alone. They beat me up mentally, and if they weren't going to take my life, I wanted to take my own. I don't know if there is anybody else out there feeling like you have no reason to go on, but I just want to say to you, you do have a reason. You've got to keep yourself together, get the right spirit, and tie yourself up with strength, so when you're attacked, you won't be destroyed. So thank you, Yuri, for helping me understand that. I guess I talked today because hopefully I can help somebody else out there understand it too."

People stood up and started clapping, even our principal, Dr. Garner, who came over,stood beside us, and took the mic. "That's right Marks High School, we're going to be victims no more. If you have evidence of anyone doing anything wrong—you all know what I'm talking about—get it to us, and it will be dealt with immediately. We're mavericks. We take the bull by the horns."

The band played as people were exiting. Logan and I couldn't get out of the place because different people were coming up to us sharing stories of feeling not only bullied, but also inferior. That made it all worth it for me to stand up and talk. More importantly, I was really happy for Logan winning her self-confidence. The best part was that texts, emails, pictures, and all kinds of testimonies and stuff about members of Onyx flooded into the office. Since we stood up, twenty-four students were permanently removed from our campus. The holidays were upon us, and that news made all of us at the school very merry.

***

Why my father insisted that I gracefully resign in person to Ms. Pinky was beyond me, and it seemed pretty excessive. I told him the lady was trifling, but yet he wanted me to thank her for the few times we worked together. Slade dropped me off, and I wanted her to wait, but she said Dad said he was coming to get me. I so hoped he was on his way as I stepped foot into Ms. Pinky's store.

As soon as I entered, Rhonda looked at me and shook her head. I knew that meant Ms. Pinky was in a mood. When was she not in one? Since I met her, something always seemed up her butt. Today I was going to pull it right out by telling her I was out and that she wasn't getting anymore free labor out of me.

Seeing me, Ms. Pinky yelled, "Chop chop, Yuri. The apron is not going to put itself on you."

Trying to be nice, I said, "I just need a second to talk to you, Ms. Pinky."

"I don't want to talk. I want to give you the orders of what I need done, and I want you to do them. We're not friends here. I'm supposed to be showing you the way. If you're not working, I can't tell you what you're doing wrong and I can't help you. I'm so mad it's Christmas season. Everyone expects a deal. Everyone comes in here all jolly. I got bills to pay, and giving them all these sales, my margins are smaller. I'm not happy, nor am I in a mood for discussion."

To her dismay, I just stood there. She was going to have to talk to me. When she wouldn't, I just looked at her. Eventually, she'd get the point and ask me what was my problem so I could tell her.

"Why are you not moving?" she screamed a few moments later.

I wanted to yell back at her, but I took a deep breath, gulped down my saliva and counted to two. Calmly, I said, "I didn't come here to work. I just came here to thank you for the opportunity for allowing me to work with you. However, I won't be doing it anymore."

"What? Your little daddy has changed his mind? Some other bakery has stepped up?"

"No, that's not it," I said to her.

Ms. Pinky scoffed, "Well what's the problem? Rhonda, tell her . . . I'm the best around. No one can teach her more than me. So what I don't baby you? You'll thank me for that."

I knew my dad was supposed to pick me up, but I was going nowhere with this lady. He was going to have to wait for me down the street at the bookstore.

"Oh, you're going to turn your back on me and walk out? Great. Get out! Don't ever come back."

As soon as I opened the door, my dad walked in with a bunch of people. I was overjoyed to see him. Now he could deal with the witch.

"Dad!" I said with excitement.

Ms. Pinky was so angry she couldn't be politically correct. She snarled at my father and said, "You and your ungrateful child. You might be our next mayor, but you are going to need the support of the people. Making alliances with business folks and then changing your mind is tacky, and I won't stand for it. I told a lot of people that we would be working together, and then you just pull your daughter before I even get to groom her!"

"Ma'am, that's the least of your worries," said an older, distinguished, white gentleman with feathered gray hair and glasses.

"What are you talking about? No riddles, I'm busy," she angrily voiced with both hands on her hips.

When I looked at my dad, wondering what was going on, he winked my way. The same gentleman said, "I am Mr. Cobb, the health inspector for the state . . ."

And before he could finish, Ms. Pinky cut him off, looked at me and said, "What she say? What she lie on me and say?"

"Maybe you can tell us," Mr. Cobb told her.

"What could you have said, you little nit whit? When they come around here to check me out I switch out some dated products? No big deal. Okay, and I might not always sell brand new baked goods, but no one has ever gotten sick. Is that what she told you I did? Is that what she said?" Ms. Pinky questioned, truly unaware of what she admitted to doing.

I was about to say that I talked to my father, but she had told on herself. When some other people by the doorway moved out of the way, two policemen asked if she could come with them. They went on to explain that there had been several complaints. She yelled out for Rhonda to help, but Rhonda corroborated all the accusations. Everything she told them about was illegal.

Hearing no backup, Ms. Pinky screamed and yelled and hollered and stomped, but she still was carried out of her beautiful place with her mean spirit. It had already started feeling more like Christmas. I hugged my father, and the health inspector thanked me. He actually commended Rhonda too for stepping up and telling the truth.

"Yeah, but I'm out a job," Rhonda said, looking somber.

My father looked at her and said, "Don't worry about that. My daughter has told me what a great lady you are. We'll find something for you at the city. Good people like you need to be working."

"But I don't have a college degree or a bunch of credentials."

"We can still find something and get you trained so you have more skills to achieve your dreams," my father told her.

"Wow, I did vote for the right person," Rhonda said while my dad humbly smiled.

The health inspector peered my way and said, "I'm glad that you want to get in this business. It's a tough place to catch criminals because lots of people want to cut corners, keep their costs down so that their profits can be wider. The culinary industry has a big job to do. Their foremost job is making sure they take care of the health of their customers. I don't want what you witnessed here to deteriorate your dreams because this place is just so beautiful, I'd hate to see it go away."

"Yeah," my dad said, quickly giving Mr. Cobb an eye to say no more. "But don't you worry about any of that. I'm proud of you."

I uttered, "I'm just glad she can't hurt

anybody anymore. Her stuff looked good, but if people knew how she made it . . . it was bad."

"Well, now we got the bad apple out the bunch. And we're working with your mother to get more out the way. Somebody's intentionally selling these bad goods. We're close. We're going to work with your father to clean up Charlotte. But with young people like you on the horizon, our future looks bright. Thanks again," Mr. Cobb said before exiting.

My dad looked at the yummy cupcakes. "Oh, but I want one so bad."

Rhonda and I looked at each other and shook our heads, no. He chuckled, but he nodded understanding. We threw all the inventory away.

***

A few days later, I was smiling from ear to ear, preparing for my sweet sixteen birthday party. It was supposed to be a surprise for Sloan and me, but both of us knew. Her birthday was two days before. While the craziness over the last two weeks had finally calmed down, I was a little melancholy as I put on my sassy, above the knee, flared out, semi-formal, hot pink dress because I hadn't heard from Paris. I'm sure he had heard the news of his aunt's arrest because it had been all over the news. But the last time we talked, we were pretty rough on each other, so I knew that was over. I had to move on.

"Oh, you look so cute!" Sloan came in and said.

She had on a tight, sparkling silver, semi-formal that was off one shoulder. It was also above the knee. Though we were two days short and two parents short of being twins, we felt like we were inseparable. Not really joined at the hip, but joined at the heart for sure. We'd been through a lot, accusing each other in certain situations, not being there for each other sometimes when we should have known better. However, the ups and downs we'd gone through over the past two months made our love for one another stronger. Maybe a part of why our relationship had gotten off track was because we never argued. Well that was sure behind us. We made up for that part and then some.

"Let's go have a great night tonight. Oh, we got to act surprised because our parents are saying they are just taking us to dinner," Sloan said.

"They better go all out."

There was a knock on my door, and it was Shelby standing there with Ansli.

"Slade's downstairs. Mom and Dad are already at the restaurant. We're going to be late."

When we pulled up at the hotel, it was familiar. It was the same place my dad held a surprise wedding anniversary party for my mom last month.

As soon as we pulled up, Shelby said, "We're just stopping here for a second."

"Okay, if we're stopping here . . ." Sloan said, winking at me. ". . . we'll wait."

"No, no, no, I need you guys to come," Shelby said.

"Well, why do you need us to come out if we're stopping here for a second?" Sloan said as I jolted her in the arm.

"Girl, get out the car," Slade said, shoving us.

We walked back to the same room my dad had the party in. I was giddy inside. I looked at my phone because it was vibrating.

It was a text from Sloan, who was right beside me, that said, "Yup, Dad must have got a two for one deal. We gonna have a nice party because you know how he set it out for Mom."

I texted back with a smiley face.

As soon as Sloan opened the door, people yelled surprise. It was so exciting to see the same beautiful room, this time decked out in hot pink and silver. Not a coincidence that my mom bought us adorable dresses that matched the color scheme she was going for with our party. It was the sassy Sharp sisters standing in the spotlight. Though my sweet sixteen was along with Sloan's, all five of us stood proud with our heads held high amongst our peers. The room was packed. There must have been three hundred kids there. There weren't the same round, sit-down tables my dad had for my mom. There was a dance space, silver and diamond and hot pink and black balloons were on the ceiling. "Happy Sweet Sixteen Sloan and

Yuri" were plastered everywhere with our pictures. I didn't even realize Ansli captured us in glam poses, but somehow she did, and we both looked like models.

My dad was on the mic and he said, "Hello young, Charlottians. Thank you all for coming to the sweet sixteen party for my daughters. This is a special time of year for the Sharp family. Not only in a month will I be inaugurated as your next mayor, but my two babies are having milestone birthdays. I no longer have little girls anymore. Officially they are sweet sixteen, and I am truly proud of the gorgeous ladies they have become."

Sloan and I hugged each other. After all was said and done, our dad was proud of us. That meant so much to us both.

We listened on as he continued, "But also Christmas is tomorrow, a special time for cheer. You guys are young, and I want to say that I hope you remember you're special. You can be anything you want to be, but take your education seriously, and go after your dreams. Don't just wait to make them come true. Make them come true now. I'm proud of my girls. So I want to introduce to you the three hosts for tonight. Ms. Shelby Sharp . . ."

Shelby had a hand held mic and said, "Hey y'all! Thanks for coming to the party for my sisters."

"How many of you guys in here have tried her clothes?" my dad said.

"Dadddd!" Shelby uttered embarrassed, but the room erupted.

"That's wassup," he said.

"Oh, you are not that cool," she told him as she gave him a kiss.

"Tonight Shelby is being escorted by her friend, Spencer." She gave her boo a kiss, and my dad said, "Alright, I approve all of that."

The two of them walked down the center aisle toward the head table.

"Then I've got my daughter, Ansli Sharp! All these beautiful pictures around here, she took them. Even tonight, she's serving her sisters. She wants to get candid shots with you guys, so make sure you go on over to the left to the beautiful display and get some pictures in about thirty minutes. Um, come on up here, Mr. Hugo. Escort my beautiful daughter."

"Thank you, Daddy," Ansli said in a shy tone.

My father coughed and said, "Not too close! Hold her hand, not her waist."

"Daaaddyyy," Ansli said.

"And then there's Ms. Slade Sharp. She'll be singing happy birthday to the girls soon. And I think somebody special who's got a hot new single out nowadays is going to perform."

When the sexy singer stepped out to escort Slade to the head table, girls screamed.

"And then there're my birthday girls."

Now I was starting to feel some type of way because before my dad could introduce Reese, Sloan's boyfriend, he walked up and stood right beside her. He said all these great things about Sloan and the two of them, and they went off to the table. Then it was just me, and I didn't have anybody to step up for me.

My dad took my mind off of that when he looked me in my eye and said, "Ya know all my girls are doing their thing. Sloan's going to be working on this magazine with me, and I know you have a passion for pastries. Well, the shop we were in the other day, you know the one I'm talking about that you think is so pretty? Your mom and I bought that, and we want to work with you on making some healthy treats. You made your dad one, and I think it's a big market to get us to indulge but to also be health conscious. What do you say? Can we go into business?"

I just hugged his neck, knowing he was going to escort me to the front. But then he said, "And I think somebody, yup, there he is, wants to escort you."

I turned, and there was Paris. We were locked arm and arm. He smiled my way, and I smiled back at him. With that gesture, the "I'm sorry" we both wanted to say melted away. Life is never going to be perfect. But Paris and I walked past our peers toward the front of the head table on my sweet sixteen birthday; my dad just told me I was going to get to make the world better with the start of my own business; my parents are fine; my dad was going to be mayor;

my sisters were fine; my grades were good; my dad was going to be taking care of himself; and I just realized the icing was on the cake, and at that moment my life was perfect.

Walking with a big smile plastered on my face, I looked over and saw Logan. She winked at me and waved, and I realized this last month had helped me develop a better backbone. I was okay without Paris, but there he was, whispering his apologies. Now I didn't just look good on the outside, but I really felt good on the inside. I'd given this self-esteem gift to myself, and that made for a special birthday and a Merry Yuletide.

ACKNOWLEDGMENTS

Special thanks to all in my life that help me put special icing on the cake.

To my parents, Dr. Franklin and Shirley Perry, you put the icing of dreaming big in my life.

To my publisher, especially photo researcher Giliane Mansfeldt, you put the icing of success in my world.

To my extended family, you put the icing of a hard work effort into my life.

To my assistants Shaneen Clay, Alyxandra Pinkston, and Candace Johnson, you put the icing of perfection into my writing.

To my friend the McHughs, for introducing me to Lerner and my first chance to write for an educational publisher. You put the icing of hope into my world.

To my teens, Dustyn, Sydni, and Sheldyn, you three give me the icing of fulfillment.

To my husband, Derrick, you put the icing of completion in my heart.

To my readers, you all put the icing of hope into my world as I hope this novel and series blesses you.

And to my Lord, you place the icing of love in my heart so that I can write stories with a purpose.